Meg Perry

Deserted to Death

A Jamie Brodie Mystery

This book is a work of fiction. Names, characters, places and incidents are either products of the author's imagination or used fictitiously. Any resemblance to actual events, places, or persons – living or
dead – is entirely coincidental.

The Jamie Brodie Mysteries

Cited to Death
Hoarded to Death
Burdened to Death
Researched to Death
Encountered to Death
Psyched to Death
Stacked to Death
Stoned to Death
Talked to Death
Avenged to Death
Played to Death
Filmed to Death
Trapped to Death
Promoted to Death
Published to Death
Cloistered to Death
Haunted to Death
Obsessed to Death
Deserted to Death

Also by Meg Perry:

The Space Coast Mysteries

Twelve Seconds
Three Thousand Miles (coming spring 2020)

Prologue

Young Research Library, UCLA
Tuesday, March 5, 2019

The rumors had been swirling around campus for weeks. The university administration's silence on the subject only served to fuel the speculation.

Layoffs.

Every local newspaper from the *Daily Bruin* to the *Los Angeles Times* had reported on the flat budgets in the university system. The president of the University of California announced at the start of winter quarter that there would be no increase in tuition or fees for in-state students in fiscal/academic year 2019/20, the second year in a row in which tuition had been frozen. It was difficult to reconcile flat budgets and flat tuition rates with the ever-increasing cost of instruction. Hence the rumors.

Nonetheless, when I received a summons via instant message to the office of my supervisor, Young Research Library director Dr. Madeline Loomis, it didn't occur to me that the rumors and the summons could be connected.

I pulled off my tie—I'd just finished a presentation to a group of faculty and administrators in the Division of Humanities—and tossed it on my desk, then hurried downstairs to the office suite. There I found my sister-in-law and fellow librarian, Kristen Beach, heading in the direction of Dr. Loomis's office as well. She stopped in her tracks and frowned at me. "You, too?"

"Yep. Any clue?"

"None." She resumed walking. "Let's find out."

We said hello to Olga Koval, Dr. Loomis's assistant, who told us to go on in. I paused and knocked anyway, and heard Dr. Loomis say, "Come."

Dr. Loomis approached us from behind her desk as we entered. She was a tiny woman with her nearly-white hair in a bun, glasses on a chain around her neck, and a pristinely clean desktop. Evidence of an ordered mind. Today she was wearing a mint green suit with a mint-and-cream striped blouse underneath. Dr. Loomis was a snappy dresser.

She indicated a group of wing chairs to our left, arranged for informal seating. "Jamie, Kristen, thanks for coming. Please, sit."

We sat. Dr. Loomis angled her chair to face both of us. "I'm sure you've heard the rumors of layoffs that have been circulating lately."

Were we being laid off? I said, "Yes, ma'am."

"Let me be clear. We are *not* laying off anyone from the library. However." She smoothed her skirt, which was already smooth. I didn't remember *ever* detecting nervousness in Dr. Loomis.

"The university has requested that academic departments offer temporary, unpaid furloughs to employees for the summer term. Let me stress, these are *entirely* voluntary. We will not force *anyone* to agree to be furloughed. But…" She paused and looked back and forth between us. "I wanted to approach both of you about possibly agreeing to a furlough. Your benefits will not be suspended. You will continue to accrue vacation days and sick leave during the furlough, and of course your health insurance coverage will not be interrupted."

Kristen and I glanced at each other. It made sense that we were asked; she and I were the ones who could afford to go without pay for an entire summer. I said, "The furlough would begin at the end of spring quarter?"

"Two weeks before. It would run from June 1 through September 15. You'd return with slightly more than a week to prepare for fall quarter."

Three and a half months of vacation. The prospect was appealing. My husband, Pete Ferguson, and I could spend extended time with our families. Dr. Loomis said, "I am accepting a furlough myself. My husband's condition has progressed to the point where he requires a caretaker during the day. We'll conserve valuable dollars of our long-term care insurance if I stay home with him this summer."

Dr. Loomis's husband had been diagnosed with Alzheimer's nearly two years ago. Kristen asked, "Will Isabel be acting director?"

Everyone in the library expected that Isabel Gutierrez would replace Dr. Loomis when she retired. Isabel had a doctorate in library science and had been a director at a community college before coming to YRL. Dr. Loomis said, "Yes. Janet Earley at Powell is also accepting a furlough, and Frida Nava will serve as acting director there."

Powell was UCLA's undergraduate library. Kristen said, "Those of us who are financially able to take furlough might be preserving other people's jobs if we accept, right?"

Dr. Loomis sighed. "If it comes to that. Yes."

I said, "I tentatively accept. I'll have to discuss it with Pete this evening, but I can't imagine he'll object."

Kristen said, "Same here. I doubt that Kevin will mind."

Dr. Loomis's expression was one of profound relief. "Thank you both *so* much. It means a great deal to me, and to Laura." Dr. Laura Madorsky was UCLA's University Librarian. "Let me know tomorrow what your final decisions are. There will be papers to sign in HR."

Kristen and I said in unison, "Yes, ma'am."

Kristen unlocked the door to her office and we both entered. I dropped into one of her visitor chairs. "Wow."

"Seriously. Think Pete will object?"

"Nope. He'll be thrilled. He'll want to spend it all in New Mexico."

"Seems like you just got *back* from New Mexico."

"I know." We'd spent ten days in mid-December at our second home in Alamogordo. "But it's a while yet until June. Do you think Kevin will object?"

"No. We won't be able to travel much, though. He's used nearly all of his leave for his field experiences."

My middle brother Kevin, AKA Kristen's husband, was on schedule to graduate from Simmons College with a master's degree in social work in early 2020. He'd be leaving his job as a homicide detective with the Los Angeles Police Department's West LA Division to work for the district attorney's office as a victim advocate, and to teach part-time at the LAPD academy.

The impetus behind Dr. Loomis's request—the reason that we could afford an unpaid furlough, the reason that Pete and I owned a second home, the reason that Kevin was able to pay for graduate school—was an inheritance. Nearly four years ago, Kevin, our oldest brother Jeff, and I had received a bequest of $38 million each from the estate of a man named Randall Barkley. Barkley's son, Gavin, had killed our mom and her friend, Tracy Jemison, in a drunk-driving accident when I was a baby and Kevin and Jeff were toddlers.

The inheritance had come as a total shock to us. Our financial adviser had said, "Don't act like rich guys," and for the most part we hadn't. Pete and I had built a house, Kevin had bought a condo and paid for graduate school, and Jeff had paid off the mortgages on his farm and veterinary practice. Even with sizable charitable donations, footing the bills for Pete's nieces' college educations, and establishing a scholarship at UCLA in honor of our dad and grandfather, we still had the bulk of the money left. And Kristen was independently wealthy herself, thanks to a divorce settlement of two million dollars from her ex, a neurosurgeon.

I said, "Old man Barkley and Doctor Daniel come through for us again."

Kristen snorted. "Right. Should we tell Liz?"

"Yeah, but let's not tell anyone else yet."

"Agreed."

We went to the second floor, where Liz Nguyen's office was next to mine. She was our political science subject specialist, and Kristen's and my best friend at work. She was frowning at her computer; her expression lightened when we appeared. "Hey, do either of you know anything about Mongolia's Third Neighbor policy?"

I laughed. Kristen said, "You're kidding, right?"

Liz sighed. “Fine. Let me send this…” She spoke the words as she typed them. “I’ll research it and get back to you.” She leaned back in her chair with a satisfied smile. “Never do this morning what you can put off until this afternoon. What’s up?”

I closed the door behind me. Kristen said, “We have something to tell you, but you have to keep it quiet for a couple of days.”

Her expression switched to one of alarm. “What?”

I said, “Dr. Loomis asked us both to take unpaid furloughs this summer. If Kevin and Pete are okay with it, we’re going to accept.”

Liz’s mouth formed an O, then she began to nod as the logic of it dawned on her. “You’re the ones who can afford it. No one’s being laid off?”

Kristen said, “Not yet. Dr. Loomis is accepting furlough, too. Isabel will be acting director.”

“*Wow.*” Liz blinked. “What will you do all summer?”

I said, “Travel, I guess.” Although I hoped that Pete would agree to spend some time at home.

Kristen said, “I have a list of projects at the house.”

“Jeez.” Liz looked back and forth between us. “These are strange times, huh?”

I said, “Indeed.”

That evening I walked through the front door of our split-level townhouse in Santa Monica and stopped in my tracks. Our yellow Lab, Ammo, bounded down the stairs from the kitchen to greet me; I ruffled his ears as I gazed in dismay at the walls of the living room. “Uh… Pete?”

No answer. He was probably upstairs in the office or bathroom. I dropped my computer bag at the door and moved closer to the nearest wall—which, like the others, was covered in sheets of paper, taped to the paint.

Each page was a section of a family tree.

I yelled louder. “Pete!”

"Coming!" I heard his footsteps as he trotted down from the top floor. He turned on the landing and said, "Hey, you're home a little early. Dinner isn't ready yet."

"Never mind dinner. What the hell is this?" I gestured to the walls.

He waved his hands, indicating the whole room. "It's impossible to get a sense of an entire family line on a computer screen. I needed to see it all in one place."

"How long are you planning to leave it there?"

"Until I reconcile it with my online trees. Maybe a week." He noted the expression on my face. "It's not like we're having company before that."

"The tape will damage the paint."

"I used the kind that won't."

I sighed, surveying the room. Once the holidays ended, Pete had jumped into genealogical research with both feet. Last winter he'd become obsessed with garden planning; once the plan was complete, he'd decided to learn everything possible about the Cahuilla Indian tribe with the intention of becoming a member, since one of his great-grandmothers was Cahuilla. He'd bought an entire library of books about the nation and been crushed when he'd learned that he wasn't eligible.

Since January, he'd bought an entire library of books on genealogy. His distant cousin in the United Kingdom, Duncan Thomson, was regularly sending him information about his Scottish ancestors. He'd visited the headquarters of the Agua Caliente Band of the Cahuilla in Palm Springs and had come away with several generations worth of information. He was teaching five online classes of abnormal psychology as an adjunct for Arizona State, Penn State, and Santa Monica College. Between teaching and genealogy, there was little time left for anything else.

Back in December, he'd admitted to me that he was distracting himself from ruminating on his life. He'd said that he felt that there was a piece of himself missing, but that he had no idea what that was. In order not to constantly dwell on it, he'd chosen to distract himself from it.

It didn't seem like a productive technique to me. But, as he kept telling me, he was the psychologist. Not me.

I scanned the room one more time, shaking my head. "Fine. One week. What's for dinner?"

I assisted as Pete threw together a meal of spaghetti with garlic bread. As we ate, I told him about the furlough.

He applauded in delight. "*Yes!* Your last day is May 31st?"

"Yep."

"We can head for Alamogordo on June 2nd. We'll accomplish *so* much at the house. This *rocks*."

"Whoa, whoa, whoa. You want to go to Alamogordo first?"

He frowned, confused. "Why not?"

"I want to go to the east coast for part of the summer. The later we wait, the deeper into hurricane season we get." Other than my dad and brothers, my entire family lived in North Carolina and Virginia.

"Oh." He considered. "But the later we wait, the hotter it gets in New Mexico."

"It'll be hot in New Mexico anyway. I'm more afraid of hurricanes."

"Okay, how about New Mexico, then east, then back to New Mexico?"

"I'd *like* to spend some time at *home*."

"We'll be home in August and September." He held up a finger. "We still have a ton of work ahead to get the New Mexico garden ready. Installing the greenhouse, planning for the beehives…"

"Yeah, okay. Will your semesters be over by June first?"

"For the most part. Yes."

I shrugged. "Fine. Alamogordo first. Why not?"

I thought the question was rhetorical.

I was wrong.

Chapter 1

Sunday, June 2, 2019
Tucson, Arizona

We left Santa Monica early. At nearly 3:30 in the afternoon we turned onto the long unpaved drive that led to Pete's family's ranch house. His sister Christine and her husband, Andy Fernandez, lived on a sprawling ranch north of Tucson with spectacular views of the mountains. Chris and her sisters-in-law operated their guest house as a combination bed-and-breakfast and dude ranch in spring, summer and fall.

Pete's dad, Jack, had moved from Lancaster, California, to Chris and Andy's ranch after a major heart attack in late 2014 from which he'd never entirely recovered. He'd been left with moderate, and gradually worsening, congestive heart failure but in spring 2018 had enrolled in a study of a new drug. During the double-blind phase of the study, we didn't know if Jack was taking the drug or a placebo, but his symptoms had abated. His stamina, color and appetite had all improved, and he'd gained a few pounds.

A couple of months ago, when the study had reached its one-year anniversary, Jack's doctor revealed that Jack had indeed been assigned to the drug group and recommended that he enter the next phase of drug testing, which would allow him to continue to receive the drug for free. Jack had readily agreed.

Jack lived in a smaller guest house, only a couple hundred yards from the main house. Or so we thought. As we drove past his house, I spotted a couple I didn't know on the front porch, who lifted their hands in greeting. I waved back. There was a car with Illinois plates in the driveway.

Hm.

We parked behind the main house. While guests were in residence, they used the front entrance and family used the back. Pete exited the CR-V and released Ammo, who bounded out and raised his leg against a mini-boulder.

Chris appeared, trotting down the steps from the back porch, and hugged us both. "How was the drive?"

Pete said, "Great, once we got past San Bernardino. Who are those people on Dad's front porch?"

"Guests." Chris's expression was unreadable. "Come in and I'll tell you about it."

We followed Chris into the house and turned right into the kitchen, which extended the length of the house from the back porch to the front. With guests at the ranch, the family ate at the farmhouse table at the rear of the kitchen, and that was where we stopped. Chris said, "Want a drink?"

We accepted glasses of lemonade. Pete said, "All right, what's going on?"

Chris took a deep breath. "We moved Dad into this house two weeks ago. We converted the office into a bedroom for him." The office was at the back of the house, across the hall from the rear section of the kitchen and had its own tiny bathroom with a shower stall. There were no bedrooms on the first floor. "We moved the desk and computer into the family room."

Pete asked, "Why?"

"He's started to forget things. Such as taking his meds like he's supposed to. Such as charging the battery on his life call button. *Important* things." She rubbed her forehead. "We had a family meeting with him and suggested that he move to the main house, and he agreed."

Pete crossed his arms, frowning. "And you didn't think to mention this to me?"

Chris rolled her eyes. "No, I didn't. I've been kinda busy. And it wasn't anything that affected you. I didn't consult Steve about it, either. We're the ones that are here with him every day that have to deal with this medication schedule and his diet and driving him into Tucson to see doctors twice a week. Not you two."

Pete opened his mouth, but I jumped in before he could escalate into an argument. "Isn't the new drug helping anymore?"

"Physically, yes. But he's experiencing these mental... glitches, for lack of a better word. His doctor said he'd seen the same effect in a few other patients in the study."

"But not severe enough to stop the drug?"

"No. He's improved so much physically... we don't want to change his medication regimen. If he's with us, it's easier to keep track of these things he's forgetting."

"It's gotta cramp your style, to some extent."

"Nah. It beats having to walk to his house every time he's due for a pill. Now..." Chris made shooing motions. "Take your bags upstairs, then say hi to Dad. He's in the family room. Then I could use your help in the kitchen."

I carried our bags to our assigned bedroom, then returned to the family room. Jack was standing, his left arm slung around Pete's shoulders in an unexpected display of affection. He smiled at me and held out his right hand. "Hey, son. It's great to see you."

I shook his hand, noting that his grip was stronger than it had been in past months. "Hey, Jack. You're looking healthy."

"I'm *feelin'* healthy. Healthier, at least." He released us both. "I guess Chris told you I've been forgetting a few details."

Pete said, "Your doctor thinks it's a side effect."

"Yup." Jack spread his hands in a "who cares?" motion. "Doesn't bother me. I'm happy to be here in the big house, and now Chris and Andy can make money off my place. It's all good."

We chatted for a few more minutes, then joined Chris in the kitchen. She presented Pete with a pile of vegetables to chop and me with a sink full of dirty dishes. I squeezed soap into the sink and said, "Jack's in an expansive mood."

"He always is." Chris removed a bowl of dough from the oven and began to mold pieces of it into dinner rolls. "Nothing bothers him these days. He's awake more during the day, and he's talked more in the past few months than he has in the past few *years*. I don't know how this drug works, but so far it's nearly *miraculous*."

Pete said, his tone of voice a bit too even, "Chris. Listen. Even though Steve and I aren't here to help, we still care what's happening. I'm not saying you need to consult us about stuff, but we'd appreciate knowing before *two weeks* has passed."

He had a point. I kept quiet. Chris waved a floury hand in the air, dismissive. "Fine. Sorry. Won't happen again."

Pete said, "You don't *sound* sorry."

She glared at him. "I *said*, it won't happen again. Okay?"

"Fine."

She huffed out an exasperated breath. Pete and I exchanged a look over her head and finished our chores in silence.

A half-hour later, Andy's sisters arrived. There were three of them, but once they descended on the kitchen it felt like double that number. Gloria, the oldest, good-naturedly banished Pete and me from the kitchen. We checked on Jack, who was napping, then headed out the back door for a walk.

I said, "As you and Chris were... um, discussing, I was imagining Jeff telling me a similar thing about Dad, being the bossy oldest who's on site with an aging parent and feels put upon as a result."

Pete snorted. "He wouldn't wait *two weeks*."

"Probably not. But the underlying dynamics would be the same."

"You and I are paying Dad's medical bills. We're putting her kids through fucking college, for God's sake." Pete's older niece, Stephanie, would be a senior nursing student at the University of Arizona in the fall; her younger sister, Samantha, was a rising junior at UCLA and was house-sitting for us this summer.

"Yes, we are."

"I'm here every month and spend an entire weekend taking care of Dad so she doesn't have to. What else does she want?"

"Maybe nothing. She has a lot going on and she was just venting."

"Not to mention, your *dad* would tell you if something similar happened with him. I was here four weeks ago, and Dad didn't say shit about forgetting anything."

“Maybe he didn’t want to worry you. Or maybe he forgot to tell you.”

“Stop making excuses for them.”

“Okay.”

He shook his head. “I swear. My family’s communication skills are fucked up.”

“No argument there.”

Chapter 2

Monday, June 3
Alamogordo, New Mexico

When we carried our bags downstairs before sunrise the next morning, packed and ready to leave, Christine handed us travel mugs of coffee and a basket full of her special cinnamon rolls. She hugged us firmly. "Text me when you get there, okay?"

Pete said, "We will. Thanks for the grub."

I added, "Yes, thank you. I want to be buried with a batch of these cinnamon rolls."

She laughed and held the door for us. "Safe trip."

Pete said, "Yes, ma'am."

As Pete and I stood together behind the CR-V to toss in our overnight bags, I said, "All is forgiven, huh?"

He snorted. "I suppose."

We drove onto our street in Alamogordo at 11:15. We'd built our one-story adobe house on two lots at the end of Las Lomas Court, a cul-de-sac, with views of the Sacramento Mountains to the east from our back patio. To the west, we saw desert scrub, a few buildings at the southern end of Alamogordo, and in the distance, the gleaming ribbon of White Sands National Monument.

We were the only house on our street so far, which suited us. We'd bought the lot across the street as well, so that our view would never be blocked.

North of us lay the bulk of the city of Alamogordo. Pete's brother, Steve, lived about a mile in that direction. A few scattered homes sat to our south as Greater Alamogordo petered out, then... nothing. Hills, scrub and desert containing a smattering of ranches all the way to the Texas border.

We raised the garage doors and parked in the driveway for ease of unloading. Meredith Lagai's car was in the third bay, but her bicycle was gone; she was at work. Meredith, Steve's ex-wife, was our full-time house-sitter until we moved here permanently. She and Steve were still friends. They'd divorced because, at the time, she worked in Albuquerque and they almost never saw each other. Four years ago, her law firm opened an office here in Alamogordo and assigned her to it, and she and Steve had rekindled their relationship.

But, fortunately for Pete and me, they weren't *quite* ready to cohabitate again.

We unloaded both vehicles, drove to the grocery store for perishables, then stopped for takeout burritos at our favorite Mexican restaurant in town. Back at home, we ate lunch on our back patio as Ammo investigated the scents in the backyard. I said, "What's the first item on your to-do list?"

"Let's build the greenhouse."

"Okay." We'd ordered a greenhouse kit two weeks ago. Steve and a couple of his friends had hauled it into the back yard for us; it was propped against the far wall, in the spot we'd set aside for it. "Building and equipping it will take several days."

"Yeah. I want it done by the time Kev and Kristen get here." Kevin was using one week of his remaining vacation to visit us; he and Kristen would arrive next Monday.

"Right."

"Then we'll paint the middle bedroom."

"Okay."

"You're so *agreeable*."

"Don't get used to it."

He laughed.

We spent the rest of the afternoon on the shaded patio listening to the sounds of our neighborhood. Ammo snoozed between us on the cool tile; both Pete and I occasionally drifted off. I brought out our binoculars and watched hawks soaring on the convection currents. Against the base of the mountains, a small plane buzzed back and forth for a while.

Far more peaceful than our tiny deck facing an alley in Santa Monica. I'd enjoy living in this house, when the time came.

Chapter 3

Tuesday, June 4

When I woke up at 6:22, Pete was still asleep, face down, his right arm slung over me. I eased out from under it; he didn't move. Ammo was dreaming, his nose and paws twitching. I quietly pulled on shorts and a t-shirt, slid my feet into sneakers, and tiptoed to the kitchen. The coffee maker was on, but there was no sign of Meredith. She was probably getting dressed.

I went through the laundry room into the garage, intending to retrieve the newspaper. I hit the button to raise the closest garage bay door and walked onto the driveway.

There was something lying in the street, against the curb across from the house.

There was some*one* lying in the street.

I ran to the person—a young man. Maybe a teenager. He was lying on his left side, his left arm stretched out underneath him as if he'd been reaching for something. He was terribly thin. Barefoot, wearing only a t-shirt and jeans. The soles of his feet were crusted with dried blood.

His eyes were half-open, clouded, unseeing. His lips were parted slightly. His hair was dark, cropped close to his head, and there was stubble on his chin and cheeks.

I bent down to feel for a pulse in his outstretched wrist, already sure of what I'd find.

He was cool.

He was dead.

I ran back to the house and into the bedroom for my phone, unintentionally rousing both Pete and Ammo, and called 911. Ammo scrambled to his feet and Pete sat up as the dispatcher answered.

"Otero County 911, where are you calling from?"

"Las Lomas Court. There's a dead body in my street." I left the bedroom, headed outside. "Ammo, stay."

He stayed. Pete followed me into the garage. "*What?*"

The dispatcher, a woman, sounded equally skeptical. "There's a *dead body* in the street?"

"Yes, ma'am. A young adult male."

"Does he have a pulse?"

"No pulse. He's cool to the touch."

"Do you know who it is?"

"No, ma'am."

"When were you last in the street?"

"Um... about 9:30 last night." We'd watched the sunset from the front porch.

I heard the first sirens approach. As the ambulance turned onto our street, Pete stopped beside me, staring at the corpse. He breathed, "Oh, my God."

The dispatcher signed off. The EMTs scrambled from their truck with equipment and we backed up into our driveway. One of them started to roll the kid over and stopped. "He's in partial rigor."

Two police cruisers parked, and an Alamogordo PD patrol officer emerged from each. They conferred with the EMTs briefly. One cop went to the body and one approached us, a burly guy with a blond brush cut. "Morning."

Pete said, "Morning."

"Officer Smallwood. What happened here?"

I told him. As he was taking notes, the other uniformed officer joined us, nodding hello. "I called the chief."

"Okay." Smallwood tipped his head toward our front porch. "You all hang out here for a while."

I said, "Yes, sir."

We retreated to the porch. I went inside to feed Ammo. Meredith was pouring coffee at the kitchen counter, already dressed for work. "Did I hear sirens?"

"Yes. There's a dead body in the street."

Her reaction mirrored Pete's. "*What?*"

"Yeah. The cops said to stay on our porch." I grabbed bananas and bottles of Coke for Pete and me. Meredith followed with her coffee cup and phone.

There were several more cars on the street, and a police car was blocking our street at its origin. Pete was sitting on the porch, focused on the activity around the body. I set the Coke on the table beside him. "Who's here?"

"Gordon." I'd met Otero County Sheriff Gordon Wayne on my first-ever visit to Alamogordo, six years ago, when TV host Dixon Gill had been discovered dead in the lobby of Steve's workplace. "And I think the guy in the windbreaker is the chief of police."

Meredith said, "Yeah. That's him."

A guy in scrubs parked down the street and went to the body. The responders milled around. Our view of the dead guy was blocked by the police chief's car.

We sat in silence for about twenty minutes. Now that the cavalry had arrived, I was having difficulty processing what I'd seen. I suspected that Pete was experiencing the same emotion. Meredith was texting, probably telling her paralegal that she was going to be late to work.

Another car parked down the street and Pete said, "There's Brian."

Detective Brian Cochrane, New Mexico State Police, was the closest thing to a trained homicide detective in this part of the state. We'd met Brian on the Dixon Gill case and had become friends. He lifted a hand in our direction, but immediately went to speak to Gordon and the police chief.

Not long after, the state police forensics unit arrived. The police chief and half of the local cops left. The other uniformed cops gathered at the end of the street. The guy in scrubs conferred with the forensics team, then they donned disposable body suits and went to work. The EMTs drove the ambulance about halfway down the street, then parked it there, opened its back doors, and sat just inside the bay, their legs dangling over the bumper.

Waiting, like us.

Nearly an hour passed. Meredith ate my banana. We still didn't talk amongst ourselves. Brian gestured to the EMTs, and they rolled a gurney to the body. When they lifted him, we saw that forensics had placed him in a body bag. The EMTs rolled the victim to the ambulance, loaded him, and drove away.

The forensics team kept working. Fifteen minutes later a pickup truck arrived; two men exited, lowered the tailgate, and opened two animal crates. A pair of bloodhounds jumped to the ground. The handlers spoke to Brian and Gordon for a few minutes while the forensics team packed their equipment and evidence. In a few minutes, I heard the approaching *whup-whup-whup* of a helicopter.

The dog handlers let the bloodhounds sniff the ground where the victim had lain. The dogs, noses plastered to the ground, led the handlers straight south, across the scrub. The helicopter approached slowly, flew right over us, and followed the dogs.

Brian strolled up our driveway. "Hell of a way to start the morning, huh?"

I said, "No shit. Want something to drink?"

"Sure."

Pete went to get a cup of coffee for Brian, who took the fourth chair on the porch and removed a notepad from his pocket. "Tell me what happened."

I provided the details. Pete returned to the porch through the front door, bringing Ammo with him, leashed, and attached the leash to the leg of our heavy wrought iron table. Brian scratched Ammo's ears. "This guy didn't sniff him out?"

Ammo was a certified cadaver dog. I said, "He didn't have the chance. If I'd let him out first, he would have."

Brian's radio crackled. "Air One to Cochrane."

"Go ahead."

"Dogs turned southeast. Just crossed South Canyon Road."

"Roger."

Meredith said, "Southeast? The dogs are heading for the mountains."

Brian's expression was grim. "Yup."

Pete asked, "Is he ID'ed?"

“No. Nothing at all in his pockets, and he doesn’t match the description of any missing persons in New Mexico or West Texas. I hope he’ll have fingerprints in the system.”

I said, “He’s not Hispanic.”

“No. That’s the first thing you’d consider—is this a Border Patrol issue? But that kid’s as white as they come.”

Pete said, “They’ll take him to Albuquerque for the autopsy?” The only medical examiner in New Mexico was located at the university medical center in Albuquerque.

“Right.” Brian drained his coffee and stood. “Thanks. I’ll see you all later.”

Meredith left, promising to bring Chinese takeout for dinner. I unleashed Ammo and allowed him to alert on the piece of ground where the victim had lain, praised him effusively, and rewarded him with treats and a long game of fetch and tug with his rope bone. One morbid bright spot in the events of the day: we’d have the scent of deceased human to train on for some time to come.

Once inside, Ammo flopped onto the kitchen floor and sacked out. Pete and I changed into work clothes and went to the back yard to construct the greenhouse.

We worked like fiends, allowing hard physical labor to drive thoughts of the dead kid from our minds, only talking about what we were doing. By the time 5:00 rolled around, the greenhouse’s exterior was complete, and we were ravenous.

Pete propped open the roof panel that would allow hot air to escape from the greenhouse, and we retreated to the patio. We were still unlacing our work boots when our phones beeped simultaneously.

I reached mine first. “It’s Brian.”

Not much new on our victim. Fingerprints not in IAFIS. Too many possibles in NamUs. He did have a tattoo on his lower spine, heart with initials TG+JB inside. Sent photo of it to state police around the country. Autopsy tomorrow morning.

Pete texted, ***Bloodhounds??***

Lost the scent at State Route 506, well south of Oliver Lee State Park. Kid must have hitched a ride and gotten out at that point.

I texted, ***What's out there?***

Not a damn thing.

Pete texted, ***Good luck***.

Brian returned a thumbs up. I said, "IAFIS is nationwide, right?"

Pete said, "Yes. Integrated Automated Fingerprint Identification System. Anyone who's ever been arrested or had a background check run for any reason is in the database. Even you and me."

"Good to know. The medical examiner will enter the kid into NamUs, right?" NamUs was the National Missing and Unidentified Persons Database.

"Yeah, after the autopsy." Pete grimaced. "For that to help, though, someone has to be missing him."

Chapter 4

Wednesday, June 5

We spent Wednesday constructing the greenhouse's water supply, which would come from four rain barrels, one on each corner of the building. Pete grilled Meredith's homemade black bean burgers for dinner. We'd finished eating and were watching the sunset on the front porch, adult beverages in hand, when Brian Cochrane's car circled to the curb. He raised a hand in greeting. "Hope I'm not interrupting anything."

Pete said, "Not at all. Want a beer?"

"No, thanks. I'm on my way home from Albuquerque but just wanted to let you know about the autopsy results."

I said, "What did it show?"

"As we expected, death was from a combination of dehydration and exposure. But there were some other findings that were—ah—disturbing."

Pete frowned. "Disturbing how?"

"For one thing, he was badly sunburned, which makes me think he isn't from this part of the country. For another, he had a few broken bones in his wrists. Matching those with other bruising, we have a theory about why the dogs lost his scent at Route 506. We think he was riding with someone and either jumped or was pushed."

Meredith said, "You're canvassing for anyone who might have seen him, right?"

"Of course. It's possible that he may have hidden in the back of a pickup truck. If so, the driver may not have known he was there. When the kid saw the main road, he may have panicked and bailed out."

Pete said, "That's not so disturbing. What else was there?"

Brian drew in a deep breath. "He had broken ribs on both sides. On the right, the fractures are consistent with jumping from a vehicle. On the left, they're older. He also had damage to both kidneys. It looks as if someone kicked him, repeatedly. And…" He grimaced. "There was significant trauma to his anus and rectum. He'd been sexually assaulted. Repeatedly."

We were silent. Pete's face was a mask. I could faintly hear traffic sounds from White Sands Boulevard, over half a mile away. Finally, Meredith said, under her breath, "Where did this kid *come* from?"

Brian shrugged. "No idea. Until we can identify him, I don't even have a *theory*."

We said goodnight to Brian. Pete, Meredith and I locked the house and gathered in the kitchen. I stacked dishes in the sink; Pete and Meredith sat on barstools. Pete asked, "Sexual slavery? Human trafficking?"

Meredith said, "I've never heard of anything at the local level. But there are a lot of places to hide in the mountains."

Pete shook his head slowly, gazing out the kitchen window to the back patio. I knew what he was thinking.

Meredith soon excused herself to review a client's file for the next day. When I finished the dishes, Pete and I retired to our bedroom.

When he was fourteen, Pete was sexually abused by his parish priest on a near-daily basis for six months. I knew that the dead kid's autopsy results were triggering terrible memories for him.

He was tugging his t-shirt over his head when I asked, "Does Meredith know?"

He blinked at me for a second but didn't have to ask what I meant. "I don't think so. Steve would have asked my permission to tell her, and he never has."

"Now that she's back in the family, maybe you'll want to tell her yourself someday."

"Maybe."

We left it at that. Pete climbed into bed and lay on his back, hands crossed on his stomach, staring at the ceiling. I slid in beside him, close but not in contact.

I knew he wouldn't want to be touched tonight.

Chapter 5

Thursday, June 6

The next morning, after breakfast, we headed to the back of the property to build the tables that would support containers in the greenhouse. Pete had been uncharacteristically quiet during breakfast; Meredith and I had chatted, avoiding the topic of the dead kid in the street.

I opened the toolbox and removed a tape measure. "You're awfully quiet this morning."

"I didn't sleep well."

"No?"

"I had nightmares."

"Shit, hon, I'm sorry."

He shrugged. "Not your fault."

"Do you want to talk about it?"

"Not particularly."

"Whenever you do, I'm listening."

He smiled weakly. "Thanks. I'm sure the nightmares will resolve."

"Did you have them before?"

"Not really."

I wasn't sure what that meant. But I let it drop.

It took the entire morning to construct the long tables. By noon we were dripping sweat, despite drinking at least a gallon of water each, but we were done. I asked, "How do you want to finish these?"

"Paint, I guess. We have plenty left over from the house interior. Not today, though."

"Oh, no. It's too damn hot. Maybe after the sun goes down."

"Yeah."

We ate sandwiches for lunch, then I took a one-minute shower. When I emerged, Pete was at his desk in the office, studying something on his computer screen. I said, "Whatcha doing?"

"Oh." He glanced up, almost guiltily. "Um. I've been thinking."

"About what?"

"Going back to school."

What? He already had a Ph.D. in clinical psychology. I circled around behind him. The website on his screen belonged to UC-Irvine. "For what program?"

"Criminal justice. Irvine has an online master's degree. It's highly ranked."

"Why?"

He shrugged. "It's just something I want to do. It's always interested me, obviously."

Pete had been an officer with LAPD for ten years before starting his doctoral studies. I asked, "Do you have time? With teaching and your genealogy research?"

"Well… I've gone nearly as far as I can with the genealogy. That project is winding down."

So, he was replacing his genealogy obsession with graduate school. I tried not to sigh and placed my hands on his shoulders. "I'm not objecting, I promise. If you want another degree, and you think you have time, that's up to you. But do you think you might be going back to school as another method of distraction?"

His shoulders tensed slightly beneath my hands. "What do you mean?"

"Well, you told me back in December that you'd used the garden planning for this house as a distraction from dwelling on whatever it is you believe you're missing in yourself. Since then you've been totally engrossed with genealogy. Now you tell me that's over, and you're jumping right into another enormous time commitment. Seems to me like you might be moving from one distraction to the next."

He shook his head firmly. "I don't think so. I've been considering this for a while. Actually…" He pointed at his screen.

"I just got the email that I've been admitted for fall. I was looking at the courses I'll be taking."

I stepped beside him so that I could see his face. "When did you apply?"

"April."

"Why didn't you mention it?"

He considered his answer for a moment. "I guess I didn't want to say anything until I knew that I'd been admitted."

It was a weak reason, but I wouldn't call him on it. He'd had enough emotional trauma yesterday and today, with thoughts of his own abuse and that of the kid in the street. "Oookay. What will you be taking?"

"Introduction to Criminology, Law and Society; Police, Courts, and Corrections; and statistics."

"Sounds fun."

He perked up, seemingly relieved. "Yeah, it does. I'm gonna order the Intro textbook so I can start reading."

"Okay." I patted him on the shoulder and left him to it, wondering if I'd ever be able to pry him away from his laptop once classes started.

Chapter 6

Friday, June 7

On Friday, we drove Ammo into town for his first appointment with his future vet.

My brother Jeff was a veterinarian with a large animal practice in north San Diego County. He'd checked the credentials of the few vets available in Alamogordo and recommended Dr. Bill Smith. Dr. Smith was older than Jeff but had graduated from the same school—UC Davis—and had done a fellowship at an animal hospital in Phoenix.

When we entered the waiting room, there were two other patients waiting—a Chihuahua in a carrier, accompanied by an elderly woman, and a large puppy of indeterminate breed who was bouncing back and forth between his humans, a mom and two young kids. At the sight of Ammo, everyone in the room sucked in a breath. The mom and the elderly lady said in unison, "What a beautiful dog!"

Pete said, "Thank you."

The receptionist stood and leaned over her partition. "This must be Ammo?"

I said, "Yes, ma'am."

The two kids were patting Ammo, much to the consternation of their own puppy, who was straining at his leash to join the fun. Mom was hanging on tightly. The older lady looked back and forth between Pete and me. I watched as she came to the correct conclusion; she sat back against the bench and drew her carrier-enclosed Chihuahua closer, an expression of taut disapproval on her face.

Hoo boy.

The receptionist handed us papers to fill out. The Chihuahua was called back, its owner sending me one final glare. The puppy was called back; his small humans said goodbye to Ammo reluctantly and followed Mom into the exam room. A middle-aged woman arrived, hauling two carriers containing a pair of the biggest cats I'd ever seen.

Cats triggered my asthma. I tried not to breathe deeply.

Fortunately, in only a couple of minutes, we were called back. The vet tech oohed and aahed over Ammo's handsomeness and walked him to the back to weigh him. When she returned she said, "Eighty-six pounds. Can he have a t-r-e-a-t?"

Pete said, "Sure."

Dr. Smith turned out to be a guy in his late fifties, his hair mostly gray, with a vaguely Southern accent. Oklahoma, maybe. He greeted us then squatted to Ammo's level. "Hiya, big guy."

Ammo panted happily. Dr. Smith ruffled his ears then stood. "You fellas are new in town?"

Pete said, "Yes. We're not moving here full-time yet, but we'll be here for half the summer, and we wanted to establish him with a vet in case of emergency."

"Sure." Dr. Smith produced a stethoscope and listened to Ammo's chest, then turned to a chart and made a note. "He's up to date on his shots, I see."

I said, "Right."

"He's on Revolution for flea and heartworm?"

"Yes, sir."

"Lift him to the exam table, if you would."

Pete hefted Ammo onto the table. "Ammo, sit."

Ammo sat, his tail swishing on the steel surface. Dr. Smith looked at his teeth, eyes and ears. "You brush his teeth?"

Pete said, "Every day."

"Well, he looks to be in super shape. Well-trained, too."

I said, "He's a cadaver dog."

Dr. Smith's interest was immediately piqued. "You don't say. Have you told Alamogordo Search and Rescue that you're in town?"

Pete said, "Not yet, since we're only here for a few weeks this time. But we will."

I said, "Although they've probably heard already."

Recognition dawned on Dr. Smith's face. "You found Danny Norman's body, back in the winter."

"Yes."

"And that dead kid. It was on your street?"

"Unfortunately."

"Do they know who he was yet?"

Pete said, "Not that we've heard."

"Strange thing." Dr. Smith shook his head. "I've been here twenty years. Nothing like that ever happened before."

I figured it was my lousy penchant for stumbling over bodies that accounted for the timing, but I thought it best not to mention that.

Fortunately, when we went to the waiting room to pay the bill, the cats—and the Chihuahua woman—were nowhere to be seen. We buckled Ammo into the car and headed home. In the passenger seat, Pete said, "I think we made the right choice."

"With Dr. Smith? Yeah."

"But what?"

"Hm? Oh. But nothing. He seems great."

"*Something* else is bothering you."

"I wouldn't say it bothers me, exactly. But the woman with the Chihuahua disapproves of the gays."

Pete turned to stare at me. "*What?* How do you know?"

"I was watching her watch us. Once she figured out we were a pair, she starting giving us the hairy eyeball."

He scoffed. "Might your imagination be working overtime?"

"Nope. You were filling out the paperwork. You didn't see her."

"I *did* see her, but I definitely *didn't* notice anything."

"Maybe your self-preservation radar is malfunctioning." I glanced at him. "You know that Otero County is politically red. And she was elderly. You must realize that not everyone we encounter is gonna welcome us with open arms."

He waved that off. "You said it, she's elderly. She's a product of her generation. I'm sure we won't run into many more like her."

"Hm. I'm not that confident."

He smirked. “Even if we do, I have no doubt that you’ll win them over with your sparkling personality.”

“Yeah, right. Let’s just be glad that she doesn’t live on our street.” Although I strongly suspected that it wouldn’t matter. I was sure that we hadn’t met our last homophobe in Alamogordo.

Chapter 7

Saturday, June 8

We were invited to dinner on Saturday evening by Russell and Mandy McCarthy. Russell was a Special Agent with AFOSI, the Air Force Office of Special Investigations, the Air Force's equivalent to NCIS. He'd been stationed at Holloman Air Force Base, just outside of Alamogordo, for ten years. We'd first met six years ago during the Dixon Gill death investigation. His wife Mandy was the sole faculty member in history at New Mexico State University-Alamogordo, the local community college.

Russell and Mandy lived a couple of miles to our north, on Scenic Drive, the main drag along the east side of Alamogordo. We left Ammo at home with Meredith—and Steve, who was visiting—and rode our bikes to the McCarthy's.

We hadn't talked to Russell and Mandy since December, so we caught each other up on events in our lives. We gathered on their rear patio, which boasted a breathtaking view of the mountains. Russell tossed chicken shish kebabs on the grill. "These will only take a couple of minutes. Hope you're hungry."

Pete and I both assured him that we were. Mandy said, "Hey, you two will be proud of me. At the beginning of spring semester, I started a GSA at NMSU-A."

A Gay-Straight Alliance. I said, "Oh, that's terrific! Was there a demand for it?"

"Yes. We started with about six students, but by the end of spring term we had around fifteen regular attendees. Enough of them are local that we're going to continue meeting through summer."

Pete said, "Congratulations. Do you meet every week?"

"Yeah. We mostly concentrate on service projects, but since you're here for a few weeks… could I convince you to be a guest speaker one week?"

"Of course. What do you want me to speak about?"

"Anything you want. Maybe start with some tips on how and when to come out to their families? We have several that haven't yet."

"Sure. I won't plan more than ten minutes, though, then we can let the students talk and ask questions."

Mandy clapped her hands in approval. "Perfect! We meet on Monday afternoons at 3:00. Can you come next Monday?"

Pete chuckled. "I think I can slot that into my packed schedule."

Mandy said, "Jamie, you could come too. It'd be fantastic for the students to see a happily married long-term couple. Some of them have been raised to believe that's not possible."

I said, "I'd love to, but that's the day that my brother and sister-in-law arrive. I need to stay home that afternoon. Some other time?"

Pete said, "We'll be here for five weeks. We'll visit the group together before we go back to LA."

Chapter 8

Sunday, June 9

We spent Sunday morning painting sample colors onto the walls of the middle guest room and debating which was the winner. On Sunday afternoon, Steve came over, and we spent the rest of the day on the patio, mostly discussing Ferguson family matters, including Jack's weird but welcome side effects from the new heart drug.

Then, talk turned to the mystery of the young man in the street.

I tried to head it off but failed. Steve and Meredith started an animated discussion of who he could possibly be, where he could possibly have come from, and, worst of all, who could possibly have inflicted his injuries, and why.

Pete didn't say a word. Steve didn't seem to consider that his brother could be stressed by the conversation. Meredith, of course, had no reason to think that he might be. She asked Pete, "What would the psychological profile be of someone who would do this?"

Pete shook his head. "It doesn't fit a recognized pattern. You know what, I'm beat. I'm gonna turn in."

Meredith was surprised. "Oh, okay. See you tomorrow."

"Yup. G'night." He went inside.

Meredith frowned at me, concerned. "Is he okay?"

"Yeah. We've been working hard physically ever since we got here. I think he's just tired."

Steve said, "You're not tired."

"I'm in rugby shape. Pete's not."

He gave me a skeptical look but plunged back into the conversation. Fortunately, it didn't last much longer. Steve left; Meredith said goodnight and went to her room, and I went to find Pete.

He was in the office, head down over a book. I rolled my chair over to sit beside him. "Whatcha reading?"

He showed me his textbook, titled *Introduction to Criminal Justice*, which had been delivered yesterday. I said, "That should be mostly review for you, right?"

"Not really. The LAPD academy doesn't cover much theory."

I hesitated, then plunged ahead. "Your brother is incredibly insensitive."

Pete snorted softly. "He always has been."

"Does he not make the connection?"

"Probably not. I bet it's been years since my abuse crossed his mind."

"I disapprove."

Pete smiled and squeezed my hand. "Of the three of us, Steve is the most like my dad. You know that Dad and I never discussed the abuse after I left for college."

"Yeah, I know. Just seems to me that such a major event should have left more of an impression on both of them."

He sighed. "They're not built that way. They are who they are."

"How does it work for Meredith, being with a guy like that?"

"Now, *that's* an excellent question. I have no idea."

I yawned. "Ready for bed yet? 'Cause I am."

"Nah. I'm gonna read for a while longer."

"Okay." I kissed him on the temple. "Don't stay up too late."

"I won't."

But he didn't come to bed until nearly 2:30.

Chapter 9

Monday, June 10

On Monday morning Pete and I rode our bikes up Scenic Drive, past the college, to Gerald Champion Regional Medical Center to meet our new doctors.

I was still seeing my LA doctor, Egan Weikal, but I needed to get established with a physician here in Alamogordo in preparation for our permanent move. If I should have an asthma emergency while we were visiting, I wanted to be able to call a doctor who already knew my history.

My appointment was for 8:30 this morning with Dr. Ryan Cotton, the only internist-pulmonologist in town. I'd learned that he was young, had been in practice here for two years, and had a good reputation.

I was glad to hear it, since I was stuck with him.

The medical center had an office building next door. Pete pushed the door open and held it as I entered. I was shocked at the frigid air that greeted me. They were spending major bucks on electricity to cool this place.

We located the stairs; I left Pete at the second floor. The doctor he'd chosen, an internist/cardiologist, was one floor above. I found Dr. Cotton's office tucked into a corner of the building. I walked into a tiny but comfortable room, as waiting rooms go. There were silk flowers on a coffee table, with magazines and a copy of today's newspaper. I went to the front desk and was greeted by a cheery young woman. "You must be Mr. Brodie."

"Yes."

"Did you fill out your health history on our website?"

"Yes, ma'am."

"Wonderful! Have a seat, and the doctor will be right with you."

I had a seat and looked around. The walls were decorated with the obligatory notices in English and Spanish, but also with gorgeous photos of the New Mexico landscape. The photographer wasn't identified.

Less than five minutes later, another young woman in a scrub suit opened the door which, I assumed, led to the exam rooms. "Mr. Brodie? Come on back."

The nurse's name was Leona. She measured my height, weight and vitals, then handed me the dreaded hospital gown. "Everything off but your briefs, please."

I undressed and took a moment to study the photos in the exam room. I'd just realized that I recognized the location when the door opened. "Mr. Brodie? I'm Dr. Cotton."

Ryan Cotton was younger than me, about six feet tall, and looked like a farm boy: fair haired, blue eyed, and muscular. I said, "I'm glad to meet you. These pictures are of Torrey Pines."

Dr. Cotton shook my hand with an astonished expression. "They sure are. Are you from San Diego?"

"Yeah. Born and raised in Oceanside. Are you?"

"Not originally, but I went to med school at UCSD and fell in love with Torrey Pines. It's where I'd go to de-stress."

"You took those?"

"Yeah. Photography's a hobby of mine." He gestured to the exam table.

I hopped up and he sat on the rolling stool by the small cart that held a laptop. "I reviewed your history. Sounds like living in Los Angeles wasn't good for your lungs."

"No. It's not good for anyone's lungs."

We discussed the triggers for my worst asthma attacks. He asked, "How have you felt during your visits here?"

"Fine. Not a wheeze."

"Have you been here during a dust storm?"

"No... are they frequent?"

"No, but the environment here is generally dusty. If the wind is blowing, there are dust particles in the air. Having said that, you're far less likely to be triggered here than in Los Angeles."

"Good."

"Your health is otherwise excellent, according to your history."

"Right."

He referred to the laptop screen. "You're married to a man."

"Yes. Happily."

He smiled, and I thought there was a flicker of something else in his eyes. *Hm.*

He asked, "Your husband is in good health?"

"He's in excellent health. He has heart disease in his family, though."

"Has he gotten established with a doctor yet?"

"Yeah. He's seeing someone in the group upstairs even as we speak."

"Good." Dr. Cotton cleared his throat. "I don't want to make you uncomfortable, but if I'm going to be your primary care physician, I have to ask you…"

"How's our sex life?"

He looked relieved. "Yes."

"It's fine. Two to three times a week. And we don't have anal sex. My husband was abused by a priest as a teenager and he's not comfortable with anal."

He winced. "That's awful. Does that create an issue for you?"

I shrugged. "At first it did, but now that I'm older—meh. It's the price of admission."

Dr. Cotton smiled knowingly. "I understand. All right, let's do your physical exam."

After my physical Dr. Cotton pronounced me fit. "Do you need prescriptions written?"

"No, I have plenty of refills."

"Okay." He wheeled back to the laptop and typed a couple of lines, then turned back to me. "I'm curious. How did you decide on Alamogordo?"

"My husband's brother has lived here for twenty years. We already have a few friends here that we've met through him."

"Ah. Any gay friends?"

“No.” I took a chance that my impression of him was correct. “I’d guess that this isn’t the ideal location for gay social life.”

He smiled wryly. “You’d guess correctly.”

“One of our friends is on faculty at the college, and she started a GSA this spring. She has about fifteen regulars.”

His expression brightened. “That’s great. There are other queer adults here, but they keep *intensely* low profiles. This is a bluish state, but Otero County is still red.”

“Yeah, we’re aware of that. We hope that people will mostly leave us alone.”

He nodded. “They mostly will. Just... be careful.”

Pete left home for the GSA meeting at 2:30, riding his bike to the college. I got the broom out and swept our living spaces; we were eschewing use of vacuum cleaners to save electricity. I was hanging the broom on its hook in the garage when Kevin and Kristen pulled into the driveway.

I pointed them to park behind the Jeep. They climbed out and we exchanged hugs. Kevin looked around the landscape. “It hasn’t changed a bit.”

“It’s the desert. How much is it gonna change?”

“True.”

I lowered the garage door and we carried their bags into the house, then moved to the back yard. I showed them the work we’d done on the greenhouse last week, and they commented on the size of the mesquite trees, which had grown since they’d visited last.

Then I told them about the dead kid in the street.

Kristen clapped her hand over her mouth, her eyes wide above it. Kevin asked, “Have they checked for similars?”

“I don’t know. We haven’t heard from Brian Cochrane since he told us about the autopsy. Surely they have, though.”

“You’d hope.” Kevin picked up his phone and started to text.

Kristen asked, “What makes you think there might be similars?”

“No reason. But there’s also no reason to assume that it’s an isolated case.” Kevin finished his text and set the phone aside. “No one's been murdered in West LA recently. Jill just wrapped up an online forensics course. This will give her something else to do." Jill Branigan was one of Kevin's fellow homicide detectives.

I said, "How long will it take her?"

"A few hours."

Pete came home bearing New Mexican food, full of excitement about his visit to the GSA. "They're a super bunch of kids. So much braver than I was at that age."

I said, "They're almost all braver now than we were at that age."

We distributed burritos and enchiladas and proceeded to chow down. We were about halfway through when Kevin's phone rang.

He glanced at the screen. "It's Jill," and answered. "Hey. Can I put you on speaker?"

She must have agreed. Kevin lay the phone on the table between us. "Did you find anything?"

Jill said, "Maybe. There have been three cases reported to law enforcement within the last year that are similar to your kid's physical condition. All three were hospitalized with bruised kidneys, broken ribs, and the same kind of rectal damage you described."

I asked, "Where were they?"

"Well, that's the problem. One was in Alabama, one was in Montana, and one was in Kentucky. None in the Southwest."

Kevin said, "How old were they?"

"Nineteen, seventeen, and sixteen."

Like our dead kid, whom I'd estimated at eighteen. Jill said, "All three recovered and were discharged home. No charges were filed. In each case, the cops were alerted by the hospital, but the victims refused to tell them anything."

"Did social services investigate?"

"If so, it was after the local cops closed the cases. The only other item of note was that all three of them had an unidentified chemical in their bloodstream."

"Were all of the chemicals the same?"

"No way to tell. The three LE agencies never talked to each other. They didn't *know* about each other."

"Okay. Thanks, Jill."

I said, "Hey, Jill, can I give your number to the investigating detective here? His name is Brian Cochrane. New Mexico State Police."

"Of course."

"Awesome. Thanks."

"You bet. Have fun this week."

Kevin said goodbye to Jill. Kristen asked, "So... what does that mean? The same injuries, but spread all over the country?"

Kevin shook his head. "With only four cases, it could be entirely random. Right now, it doesn't mean anything, unless your local guys can find out where your kid came from."

With an entire mountain range to search, I had doubts that anyone could locate the origin of our dead kid.

Chapter 10

Tuesday, June 11

When Kevin and Kristen had honeymooned at our house, they'd gone to Roswell and Carlsbad but hadn't spent much time exploring Alamogordo. Not that there was much to explore... but we'd planned a walking tour of the town for this morning, to orient them to our new city.

We were up early, intending to beat the worst heat of the day. While Pete made breakfast, I went through the garage to get the newspaper and found it in its usual spot at the end of the driveway, encased in a plastic wrapper. I lowered the garage door behind me and joined the others on the patio, upturning the wrapper to allow the newspaper to slide onto the table beside Pete. As I did, a separate scrap of paper fluttered to the tile under my feet.

It appeared to be a lined sheet of notebook paper, folded into quarters. I bent down to pick it up, and Kevin scrambled to his feet. "Don't touch it."

I froze, halfway down, and craned my neck to look up at Kevin. "Why?"

"Because it shouldn't be there. Where's the nearest box of tissues?"

Pete said, "Guest bathroom."

Kevin disappeared into the house. I straightened up but didn't move. Pete, Kristen and I stared at the sheet of paper like it might explode. I said, "He's just being abnormally cautious, right?"

Pete said, "Sure."

Kristen said, "It's probably just a note from your carrier."

Kevin returned with the box and pulled two tissues out. He draped them over his fingers and picked up the paper, laid it on the table and carefully unfolded it.

The message was handwritten in capital letters with a red Sharpie.

NO QUERS IN ALAMOGORDO

GO BACK TO SANFRANSISCO
OR YOUL'L BE SORRY

Kristen sucked in a breath. I said, "*Fuck.*"

Pete moved beside Kevin, where he could study the note from the proper angle. Kevin asked him, "Thoughts?"

Pete's tone was analytical. Detached. "Misspellings indicate lack of education. Use of the word queer indicates someone that's too old or too out of the mainstream to realize that it's not considered an insult anymore."

Kevin said, "Do you know who's friendly in the Alamogordo PD?"

Pete said, "Not yet. But Steve would."

"Call him."

Pete went inside to call Steve. Kristen said, "This is *outrageous*."

I pinched the bridge of my nose. "Dr. Cotton was right."

Kevin said, "What?"

I told him and Kristen what my doctor had said. Pete stepped back onto the patio as I said, "Then he said, 'be careful.'"

Kevin grunted. "Good advice, apparently."

Pete said, "Steve's calling a friend of his who's a detective with APD. They'll be here in about twenty minutes."

Kristen said, "I'd better get dressed." She went inside.

It was closer to a half hour later when Steve parked at the foot of our driveway, accompanied by a man in a separate car whom I'd never seen before. I opened the front door to them. Steve said, "This is Tobias Rice. Tobias, this is my brother-in-law, Jamie Brodie."

Tobias Rice was about my size, a shaved-bald African-American man wearing an APD polo shirt, jeans, and a shoulder holster, and carrying what I figured was an evidence case. I shook his hand. "Thanks for coming."

"Glad to help." His voice was low but powerful. "Where is this note?"

"Right through here." I led him into the house and to the patio.

Tobias greeted the others, then snapped on a pair of latex gloves and lifted the sheet of paper, examining it from all angles. "Tell me how you found this?"

I told him. He asked, "And this was when?"

"About 45 minutes ago."

He thought out loud. "Newspapers are delivered around 5:00-5:30. You find it an hour or so later…"

Pete said, "Easy for someone to go unseen in the dark."

"Yup." Tobias nodded at Ammo. "The dog didn't hear anything?"

I said, "The house was built to be soundproof."

He unlatched his case and extracted a fingerprinting kit. Several minutes later, he had a full set of clear prints. "I'll run these through IAFIS, see what pops. Anything else unpleasant happens, you call me direct." He recited his number, which both Pete and I copied into our phones.

Pete saw Tobias out, then returned. Steve said, "Tobias is the only black cop in Otero County. His wife teaches math at the high school. They live down the street from me."

I said, "I didn't know that APD had any detectives. Why didn't he come when we discovered the body?"

"He doesn't have any training in homicide investigation. I think APD prefers to let the state police handle those cases. But he has plenty of experience in evidence collection." Steve punched Pete lightly in the shoulder. "I'm late to work. See ya."

Pete followed Steve outside. I turned to Kevin who was standing at the edge of the patio, his arms crossed, frowning at me. Behind him, Kristen was pacing. I said, "What the *fuck?*"

Kevin said, "This is unacceptable."

"I'm open to suggestions. But there's nothing we can do about it, is there? Other than calling the cops?"

"No."

Kristen was still pacing. "Maybe Jeff and Colin shouldn't visit."

Jeff and his eldest, my nephew Colin, were scheduled to visit next week, arriving the day after Kevin and Kristen left. I said, "Then the terrorists win."

"True. But what if the attacks escalate?"

Pete came through the back door as she spoke. "They won't."

Kevin said, "You don't know that."

"No, but I can predict it. Whoever these people are, they've done the worst they can think of."

"Are you fucking *kidding* me?" Kevin waved his hand in the general direction of town. "This county is loaded with right-wing Second Amendment fans. You can't say that someone isn't out there planning a drive-by."

Pete scoffed. "Seriously? This is a small town. Nobody's going to try anything like that."

"You think shit like that doesn't happen in a small town? You *grew up* in a small town. You *know* how unpleasant the local yokels can be."

I'd inched my way to stand beside Kristen, and we watched as Kevin and Pete argued. It was a new experience for me. Finally, Pete said, "You're overreacting."

Kevin wasn't done. "And you're sticking your head in the sand. Don't be naïve. Did you think this rural county would be gay-friendly? Would happily live and let live? Would give you a pass because you're Steve's brother? What *do* you think?"

Pete was attempting patience, but I could tell he was gritting his teeth. "I. Think. That. It. Will. Be. *Fine*."

Kevin stared at Pete for a minute, and I realized something that I never had before. I'd thought them equal in terms of intimidation factor, but I'd been wrong.

In a contest of wills, Kevin would always win.

Kevin lowered his voice. "You and Jamie can take care of yourselves. But I am not going to allow Jeff and Colin to walk into the middle of a dangerous situation."

"That should be Jeff's decision."

"It will be, as soon as I explain it to him." Kevin strode into the house, closing the patio door firmly behind him.

Pete said, to no one in particular, "He's overreacting."

I said, "I'm not convinced of that."

He shifted his gaze to me. "You, too?"

"Pete. We've been *threatened.* Sure, it might not happen again, but I agree with Kev. I'm not willing to risk Colin to that chance."

Kristen looked back and forth between us. I waited. Eventually, Pete blew out a deep breath. "I'm going for a walk."

Kristen said, "I need a drink."

I said, "Me, too."

When we went into the house, Kevin was in the family room, pacing just as Kristen had, while he talked to Jeff. Kristen and I got bottles of Coke from the fridge and cracked them open. I was taking a long drink when Kevin came into the kitchen, holding out his phone. "He wants to talk to you."

I took the phone and said, "Hey."

Jeff said, "Is Kev overreacting?"

"Pete thinks so. I don't necessarily agree."

He sighed. "Colin was super excited about coming to Alamogordo again."

"I know. It's your decision."

"I'll talk to Val tonight. We'll let you know."

"Okay."

"And for God's sake, *be careful.*"

"I will. Don't tell Dad about any of this."

"God, no."

I said goodbye and handed the phone back to Kevin. "He and Val will discuss and decide."

Kevin said softly, "I'm not overreacting."

"I know." I set my bottle on the counter and rubbed my face. "This whole adventure was originally my idea, you know."

Kristen asked, "How so?"

"When we inherited the money and I first thought of building a second home, same-sex marriage wasn't legal at the federal level yet. But it was already recognized here in New Mexico." I counted on my fingers. "My criteria were no earthquakes, no wildfire, and that our marriage would be valid. And Steve was here, and all the elements necessary for solar and geothermal living. It seemed perfect."

Kristen said, "Eventually, it'll be all right. I think. But it'll be easier if you rapidly establish yourselves as Those Who Must Not Be Fucked With."

Kevin snorted. "You'll enjoy that."

I clinked my bottle against his. "*Hell*, yeah."

We went for our walking tour after breakfast, operating under an unspoken agreement not to mention what had happened this morning. We visited Meredith's office and said hello to her and Del Chee, her legal assistant; went into the public library, then walked toward the park on White Sands Blvd. On the way, we passed the New Mexico State Police building. I said, "I wonder if Brian has talked to Jill yet?"

Pete sighed, a deep, aggravated sigh, but didn't respond. Kevin said, "Probably."

We didn't discuss further.

Back at the house, Pete and Kristen went to work in the kitchen—Pete had promised to teach Kristen to make mole poblano. Kevin and I went to the back yard to sand and stain 1x8s, intended for the construction of a bookcase in the basement.

Since we'd had nothing but sun for a couple of weeks, with more in the forecast, we decided that we had enough electricity stored to use the electric sander. I ran an extension cord from an outlet on the patio and manned the sander, while Kevin cracked the lid on the can of wood stain and got busy.

Before long we were about halfway done and had a row of stained boards drying in the sun, propped against the wall that surrounded the back yard, which we'd draped with tarps to prevent being stained. I said, "Great work. This calls for a Coke."

Kevin said, "No argument here."

I went inside—Pete and Kristen were still at the stovetop, and the house smelled divine—and retrieved Cokes from the fridge. When I went back to the patio Kevin was sitting on the edge of one of Pete's raised beds, the sun at his back. We saluted each other with our bottles then drank deeply. Kevin asked, "Are you worried about the homophobia here?"

"Not worried, exactly, although it's a concern. I think…" I realized as I spoke that it was true. "In the back of my mind, I expected it, although I hoped it wouldn't be as out in the open as it seems to be so far. I knew this was a red county, but I guess I thought it would have more of a libertarian bent. Leave us alone, and we'll leave you alone."

"Maybe there's only a handful."

"Yeah, but how much trouble will the handful be?"

"Good question."

"On top of that... I don't believe that Pete was expecting anything but open-armed welcome. Steve has lived here for twenty years, after all, and we've stayed here before for up to a month at a time. And no one has ever said anything."

"How much interaction with the townspeople have you had in the past, though?"

"Other than picking up takeout at restaurants? Not much."

"And who among Steve's friends and neighbors already knew that Pete was gay?"

"My guess? Not many."

Kevin shot me a sideways glance. "Pete's not as skilled at handling anti-gay sentiment as you are."

I thought back to my confrontation with the homophobic West LA cops at Elias Pinter's going away party, a year and a half ago. I said, "Brendan Noonan and his pals tortured Pete for a year and he never did anything about it."

"No, he didn't. You finished them off in three minutes."

"Why did he never stand up for himself?"

Kevin propped his elbows on his knees, rolling his bottle back and forth between his palms. "I always wondered. Part of it, I suppose, was that he relied on me to defend him. But I wasn't always around. The locker room was the worst."

"He's told me a little bit about that."

“He thought the best way to deal was to not react. To let it roll off him.”

I said, “That’s not how he’s built. Shit doesn’t roll off. It soaks in.”

“Yeah. I knew he was internalizing it, but I didn’t know what to say.” Kevin flipped his bottle in the air and caught it. “Now, I’ve learned enough about counseling, I might be able to help him.”

“If he’ll let you.”

“There is that.” He set his bottle to the side and stood. “Let’s finish these boards.”

We ate refried beans and rice for dinner, with chicken cooked in the mole poblano, then sat on the patio with beer bottles in hand and discussed Pete’s plans for the garden while we waited for the stained boards to dry completely. I was checking them again, determining that they were dry enough to bring to the patio, when I heard Pete’s phone and mine both beep with texts.

Pete was already responding when I reached my phone. Brian Cochrane had texted, ***Are you guys home?***

Pete answered, ***Yes.***

I have news. Can I swing by on my way home?

I jumped in before Pete could say no. ***Sure.***

Cool. See you in ten.

When Brian arrived, he accepted a beer and joined us on the patio. “I spoke to Jill Branigan this morning, then called the cops in each of the locations where the similar cases had reported. They emailed me the case files.”

Kevin asked, “What was in them?”

“Not much more than we already knew. The injuries that the kids presented with were identical to what we found on our victim’s autopsy. Other than the broken wrists, which we think our victim got by jumping out of a moving vehicle.”

Pete asked, “Have you decided he wasn’t pushed?”

Brian shook his head. “It’s still possible. But we set up a roadblock on State Road 506 near the intersection with 54 and stopped everyone that came through for a 24-hour period. Most of the vehicles were pickup trucks. Some of them travel that stretch of road every day, back and forth between Piñon and the highway. None of them saw anyone of our victim's description, but several said that they could have had a hitchhiker in the truck bed and not realized it."

Kristen asked, "What's in Piñon?"

"About seventy people and a post office. No place remotely that our victim could have come from." Brian drained his beer. "We might catch a break tomorrow, though. I heard from an Indiana State Trooper today, who thinks he might know who that tattoo belongs to. I'm driving to Albuquerque tomorrow to Skype with him at the medical examiner's office."

Kevin asked, "What about the victims in the other states?"

"The one in Montana is over eighteen. I'm flying up to meet him on Saturday. He wouldn't tell the local cops anything, but he sounded willing to speak with me."

I said, "Fingers crossed."

Chapter 11

Wednesday, June 12

The next morning, at breakfast, I got a text from Jeff. ***Val doesn't want us to come. I tend to agree, especially for Colin.***

I understand. Did you tell Col why?

Yeah. He's unhappy, but he gets it.

Okay. Some other time.

For sure. You all be careful.

You bet.

Pete was watching me. I said, "Val and Jeff have decided that now is not the time for Colin to visit."

Kevin, wisely, remained silent. Pete's face was dark, but he was externally calm. "So your nephews will never visit?"

I said, "Now who's overreacting?"

Kristen said, "Once you figure out who's behind this and neutralize them, I'm sure it'll be fine."

"*Neutralize* them?" The volume of Pete's voice rose slightly. "*Seriously?* This is not a *war*."

Kristen crossed her arms and narrowed her eyes. I thought, *Uh oh*. She said, "You're being forced to fight to be accepted and respected in this town. What would you call it?"

Pete snorted. "This episode is an anomaly."

"There are thirty-three churches here that are Baptist, Fundamentalist, Church of God, etcetera. *Thirty-three*. Not that anomalous, I bet."

"You *counted churches?*"

"I sure did. I wanted to know what you were up against."

I sidled over to stand by Kevin as we watched Pete and Kristen argue. I didn't have to wonder who would prevail in a contest of wills between *them*. Pete's volume increased by another notch. "Unbelievable. This is not even your *business*."

"No? Being concerned for my family is not my business? Wanting my brothers-in-law to be safe is *not my business?*"

"*There is nothing to worry about!*"

"And you are in *complete fucking denial!*"

I held up my hands. "Whoa, whoa. Can we table the discussion?"

Kristen said, "Fine by me."

Pete didn't respond. He shoved past us and went out the back door.

Kristen watched him go. "Sorry."

I said, "Don't apologize. I appreciate your concern. Pete will, too, as soon as he chills out."

"I'm not wrong."

I sighed. "No. I'm afraid you're not."

Kevin helped me clean the kitchen, then he and Kristen went to the front porch. I poured water from a jug into a bottle and went out back to find Pete. He was in the far southeast corner, opposite the greenhouse, chopping at a hardened section of ground with a mattock. I leaned against the wall and watched him. Finally, he stopped, dripping with sweat, and glared at me. "What?"

"Nothing. What are you doing?"

"This is where the beehives will sit. I'm leveling this piece of ground."

"Do bees need flat ground?"

"No idea. But our bees will have it."

"Lucky bees."

He blew out a breath and stared at the sky. "This is not how I wanted my summer to start."

"Me either." I handed him the water bottle.

He took a long drink. "Someone's trying to frighten us. Or provoke a response."

"I'm sure they are. But there's a difference between us not responding, and us completely ignoring the threat."

"What do you propose that we do?"

"Proceed with caution. Do everything we planned while watching our six."

"We *planned* to have Jeff and Colin visit."

I sighed. "Pete, you're not a parent. Jeff and Val are protecting Colin. That's what parents do."

He kicked at a loose clump of dirt. "Not mine."

"Let me rephrase. That's what *good* parents do."

"Steve will be disappointed."

"Steve will *understand*." Probably.

He looked around the property. "I love it here."

"So do I. But aren't you glad we have an eight-foot wall?"

He grimaced. "And it was your idea. I didn't think we needed it."

"My intent was to keep critters out of our vegetables and allow us to walk into the back yard naked if we wanted to. I didn't realize we'd need protection from anything but coyotes."

"I refuse to build a moat."

I laughed. "That would drain the well, for sure."

"I've never argued with Kristen before."

"I don't recommend it."

He snorted. "I can see why."

I wielded a level to complete Pete's bee preparation, then we went inside. Pete headed for the shower. I took a Coke to the front porch, where Kevin, Kristen, and Ammo were sprawled in various poses. Kristen craned her neck to look at me. "Everything okay?"

"Yeah. He broke up some hard-packed ground in the back. He's in the shower now."

Kevin said, "We didn't mean to be the guests who came to argue."

I waved that off. "All of it needed to be said."

Kristen asked, "Why is Pete being so stubborn?"

"Do you *know* him? He *is* stubborn. But I also suspect that he really wasn't expecting to have to deal with in-our-faces homophobia."

Kevin said, "It's not only stubbornness. This harassment is crashing into his vision of what living here would be like."

"*Yes*. He's constructed this idealistic vision of our future in Alamogordo."

"He thought he could leave the troubles of his past behind. That moving here would be a fresh start for him."

"Christine pointed out to him in December that this town could be a sister city to Barstow. He didn't like that. But now he's seeing that she was right, and he doesn't want to accept it."

Kevin said softly, "You have to brace yourself for more homophobia."

"Oh, believe me. I'm expecting more."

Kristen asked, "What will Pete do then?"

I shook my head, gazing into the distance. "I don't know."

Chapter 12

Thursday, June 13

Kevin and Kristen had decided to visit Ruidoso for the day. A wise decision, I thought, allowing more time for de-escalation of tension between Kevin, Kristen, and Pete.

I leashed Ammo and we went out the front door, locking both it and the screened gate behind us. I was just turning around when Pete said, "Who's that?"

There was a car parked in the circle, and a man standing across the street at the site where the victim's body had lain. He was staring at the ground, one hand over his mouth. He seemed to be crying.

He heard us as we approached him and turned, wiping his eyes. Pete said, "Can we help you?"

"No. I mean… no, thank you. I'm okay."

He clearly wasn't okay. I said, "Are you sure?"

He blinked, and tears coursed down his face again. "I'm sorry. I just…" He waved his hand at the ground. "Jacob was my…um…friend."

Pete said, "Jacob?"

"Jacob Baldwin." He suddenly seemed to realize where we'd appeared from. "*Oh*. Was it you that…"

Ah. Our victim had apparently been identified. Pete said gently, "Yes. I'm Pete, and this is my husband, Jamie."

At the word *husband*, the guy's eyes widened. "You're married? To each other?"

I said, "Right."

He dissolved into tears again. "Oh my God. Jacob and I were… We'd dreamed about getting married someday. We used to talk about running off to California. We…" He began to sob.

Pete said, "We're so sorry for your loss."

"Thank you." The guy—he was just a kid, really, not far out of his teens—swiped angrily at his cheeks. "Everyone here has been so nice. And now Jacob's family will sweep in and take charge, and…" He started crying again.

Pete said, "What's your name?"

"Travis. Travis Green." He struggled to regain control. "My sister's husband is an Indiana State Trooper. He happened to see the photo of Jacob's tattoo that the police here sent out, and thought he knew whose it might be. He and my sister showed it to me." He took a long, shuddering breath. "I *knew*. I *knew* something bad would happen."

I said, "Why don't you come up on the porch?"

"Don't you have to walk your dog?"

Ammo had completed his business while we'd been talking. I said, "He's done the important stuff. Come on, let's sit down."

Travis trailed us to the porch. Pete said, "Can I get you something to drink? Water, juice, tea, Coke? Something else?"

"Coke would be great, if it's not too much trouble."

"No trouble at all." Pete hustled into the house.

I wrapped Ammo's leash around the arm of my chair. "Why did Jacob come here?"

"It was a church camp of some sort." Travis sniffed, hard. "His parents wanted him to go into the ministry. This was supposedly a training site for church camp counselors."

Pete returned, bearing a bottle of Coke, a box of tissues, and the wastebasket from our bathroom. Travis accepted them gratefully.

I said, "It was *supposedly* a training camp? Was there any indication that it wasn't?" Of course, Jacob's autopsy had indicated that it probably wasn't, but I wouldn't mention that. I doubted that Travis would have been told the details of Jacob's condition.

"No. It's just that we searched for information about the camp, and there wasn't anything online that we could find. Not even a *mention*, much less a website. We were suspicious, but there wasn't much we could do."

Pete asked, "Why not?"

Travis sighed. "Jacob hadn't come out to his parents, but we think they suspected that he was gay. They were horrible.

Controlling and hateful. They had to know where he was and who he was with all the time. I mean, we're twenty years old. We're not kids anymore. But Jacob still lived at home, so he kinda had to do what his parents said."

I said, "They were religious fundamentalists, I take it?"

"Yeah. Evangelical Baptists." Travis blew his nose. "My parents are too, but when I came out and my parents kicked me out my junior year of high school, my sister and her husband took me in. My sister's ten years older than me. She's always protected me."

Pete said, "That's good. You've got family support."

"Yeah. Jacob didn't have any." Travis twisted a tissue between his fingers. "He was on schedule to graduate from community college at the end of fall term. As soon as he had his degree, we were planning to leave town. When this camp thing came up… I was afraid that his parents were having him kidnapped into some cult or something. But Jacob wasn't worried. He said it was just one more thing we had to get past."

I asked, "Did you hear from Jacob while he was at the camp?"

"No. He said he'd text me when he got to the camp, but he didn't. I texted him every day for six weeks, but he never responded."

I said, "Maybe the campers had to give up their phones while they were there."

Pete added, "Or they didn't have reception up in the mountains."

"I guess." Tears rolled down Travis's cheeks again. "Jacob was always so optimistic. His life was so much lousier than mine, but it was him that kept me going. What am I gonna do now?"

Pete asked, "What would Jacob have wanted you to do?"

Travis thought about that for a moment. "Finish college, I guess. Move away and have a *life*."

Pete said gently, "Then you can honor Jacob by doing that."

I asked, "Did you fly to Albuquerque?"

"Yeah. The medical examiner was awesome. He let me see and identify Jacob, but then he explained that he'd have to call

Jacob's parents, since they were his next of kin. He apologized for having to do that, but I understood." Travis's mouth twisted. "I had to leave Albuquerque before Jacob's parents got there, but I wanted to see where… Detective Cochrane gave me the address, so I rented a car and drove down here."

Pete said, "Are you going back to Albuquerque?"

"No. I don't want to run any risk of seeing the Baldwins. I'm going to fly home from El Paso tomorrow."

Despite his grief, Travis hadn't lost his ability to think straight. I said, "That's smart."

"Thanks." Travis looked back and forth between Pete and me. "How long have you been married?"

I said, "Four years." Almost.

He smiled weakly. "That's awesome. It's...hopeful, you know?"

Pete smiled back. "There are a lot of us out here, living perfectly ordinary lives. Don't ever lose sight of that."

"I won't." Travis blew his nose one final time and drained his Coke. "I should go. But… Do you know who owns that lot?"

Pete said, "We own it. Are you thinking about a memorial of some sort?"

"I was. But I didn't bring anything with me, and I don't know whether the Baldwins are gonna come down here. I wouldn't want them to see that someone else had been here."

Pete said, "Jacob walked here from the base of the mountains. We could show you approximately where that was. It's on your way to El Paso, anyway."

Travis brightened a bit. "Oh, that'd be great. Thank you *so* much. But I still don't have anything to leave there."

I said, "How about some stones? You can arrange them however you like."

We let Travis choose several rocks from the pile in the far corner of our back yard that had been left over from construction. Then, after he'd stood for a few more moments at the site of Jacob's death, we got into our respective cars and led him south on

U.S. 54 to its intersection with Route 506. We turned toward the mountains, not knowing exactly where Jacob had left his ride, and stopped about five miles from the main road, just into the foothills, the first spot where Jacob could conceivably jump out of a truck bed without being seen.

Travis went to work in silence, carefully constructing a small cairn about twenty yards from the road, at a spot where no one was likely to notice or disturb it. He stood back and asked, "What do you think?"

Pete said, "It looks right to me."

"Me too." Travis snapped a couple of photos of his creation, then turned to us. "Thank you both so much for everything. I appreciate it more than I can say."

I said, "We're so sorry for everything you've been through."

"Thanks. If you ever drive out this way again, will you check on this?"

"You bet."

Pete said, "Why don't you take my phone number? In case you ever want to get in touch about anything again."

Pete and Travis exchanged numbers. We said goodbye and led him back to U.S. 54. He turned south toward El Paso, and we turned north toward Alamogordo.

Chapter 13

Friday, June 14

Kevin and Kristen had gone to visit the petroglyphs and lava flow. Meredith had gone to work. Pete was in the office, reading. I decided to sweep the front porch—even without dust storms, dust collected on outdoor surfaces—and went out through the garage, grabbing the broom on my way. I was about half finished when a car pulled up across the street, exactly where Jacob Baldwin had ended his journey.

A middle-aged couple emerged. The man put his hand over his eyes and scanned the area. The woman walked along the curb, staring at the ground.

Jacob's parents, I suspected. Indirectly responsible for his death, having sent him away to some alleged church camp. I ignored them. After about a half a minute, though, they conferred briefly then approached me.

The couple vaguely resembled each other. Doughy faces, dark hair, dumpy bodies. The man said, "Excuse me. Are you the one who discovered the...the body across the street?"

I set the broom aside. "Yes, sir."

The wife spoke up. "Could you point out the exact spot to us?"

I said, "You're parked on it."

The woman gasped. "Allen, move the car!"

The man grumbled but did as she asked, backing the car up several yards. The woman said, "Can you show me?"

"Sure." I walked with her to the end of the driveway and showed her to the spot where Jacob's body had lain, then stepped back.

She knelt, rubbing her hand over the ground. A low keening sound floated up to my ears.

The man—Allen—approached. "Mary Lee, that's not necessary."

She whirled on him with sudden fury. "Don't you tell *me* what's necessary! *You* said it was necessary for Jacob to come here! He's dead because of *you!* This is *your fault!*"

Whoa. Allen winced. "Mary Lee…"

She held up a hand. *Stop.*

I backed away, but Allen turned to me, looking for support. "Could you tell... Did he suffer?"

Had they not received the autopsy report? I allowed the tiny amount of sympathy I felt for them to be overruled by the sudden surge of anger at what they'd done and said, "Yes, sir. I believe he did."

Mary Lee cried out as if I'd stabbed her. I supposed that I had. I wished that I felt worse about it. Despite what she'd said to Allen, I was sure she'd been compliant in her son's visit to...wherever he'd been.

Allen's face twisted. "This wasn't how… We weren't…"

I crossed my arms and clamped my lips shut. Otherwise I was likely to say something that all of us would seriously regret.

Allen turned away from me. "Mary Lee…"

She held up her hand again.

Allen turned back to me. "The police won't tell us anything. Do you know… Have they said anything to you…"

They had, but I wasn't about to tell him. "No, sir. I think that's standard procedure in an ongoing investigation."

That got Mary Lee's attention. "Ongoing investigation? Into *what?*"

I said, "Well, ma'am, the detective who spoke to us was a homicide investigator."

She gasped. "*Homicide?*"

Allen snapped, "They told us this, Mary Lee."

So I wasn't overstepping my bounds. She cried, "He died of *exposure*. They *said* so."

Allen said, "Complicated by the injuries he had. Someone at that place beat him, Mary Lee."

She'd been kneeling at the curb; now she collapsed into a sitting position and began rocking back and forth. "Oh, dear Lord, help me…"

I said, "I'll leave you two alone."

Allen reached out and grabbed at my sleeve; I stepped away, out of his reach. He said, "No. Please. You're the last one to see him."

Not really. I said, "Sir, he wasn't alive when I found him."

"No. I know. But…you saw him. You were with him for that short time."

I asked, as if I didn't know, "What was his name?"

"Jacob." Allen's face twisted again. "Jacob Mark Baldwin."

I said, "Mr. Baldwin? What on earth was Jacob doing out here?"

Allen gulped. "He… We'd sent him to camp. Jacob was confused. He needed help to get his life back on track."

"Confused?"

"Yes. He…" Allen eyed me, probably wondering what kind of audience he had. "Are you a man of faith, Mr. - err…"

"Brodie. Jamie Brodie. And no, sir, I'm not."

"I see." Allen wasn't sure what to do with that. He looked at my left hand and saw my wedding ring. "Well, but you're a *married* man. You must know that there are men who—err—aren't like us."

I thought, *Easy, Jamie. He's a grieving parent. Don't get into it with him.* I said, "You're speaking of gay men."

"*Yes*. Jacob was battling...unnatural urges. This camp was a place where he could learn to overcome those urges. Where he could learn to be *normal*."

Oh. My. Fucking. *God.* These people had sent their kid to a fucking *conversion* camp. I gritted my teeth and said, "Conversion therapy is illegal in New Mexico." Only for minors, but I wouldn't add that detail.

Mary Lee had grown quieter. She was still sitting by the curb, swaying back and forth, but I thought she was listening. Allen seemed genuinely shocked. "It *is?*"

"Yes, sir. The people running this camp were breaking the law." In more ways than one.

Allen blinked. "Well. There is a higher law than man's at work."

I wasn't going to let him get away with that shit. "Sir, do you support law enforcement?"

He drew himself up. "Of course. Our police are heroes."

"I agree. My brother is a police officer. And I can tell you that he, and all other law enforcement officers, do not recognize or respect any law other than the law of the land. The people who run that camp are criminals, and they will be brought to justice."

Allen's eyes narrowed. "If it be God's will."

That seemed to be the last straw for Mary Lee. She scrambled to her feet and got in his face. "Allen, *shut up*. Do you believe that it's God's will for our baby to be *dead?* For him to have suffered at the hands of *criminals?* Was it God's will for us to take out a second mortgage that we'll never be able to pay back and hand all that money over to *criminals?* Do you *hear* yourself?"

Whoa. I blurted out, "A second *mortgage?*"

Mary Lee's eyes were flashing. "Yes. The enrollment fee for the camp—for this *illegal* camp—was $50,000. For every week that Jacob stayed there, it cost us another $5,000. He was there for six weeks. *Eighty thousand dollars*. And what do we have to show for it? A *dead child*." Her voice broke and she began to cry. "My baby. My sweet baby boy..." She collapsed to the ground again.

At the words *eighty thousand dollars*, my jaw had dropped. *Somebody* was getting filthy rich off deluded parents. Allen looked ten years older. "She's right. We'll never be able to pay back the loan. We own a shoe shop. We're barely making ends meet as it is. We both have second part-time jobs, but they don't pay much." He shook his head, staring into the distance. In the direction from which his son had crawled onto my street and died.

Mary Lee said, almost to herself, "We're ruined."

I said, "I'm sorry." And I was. But sorry only for Jacob, who'd desperately tried to save himself from the hell his parents had consigned him to. “I should get back to work. Stay as long as you like.”

Mary Lee stood up again, her face tear-streaked but her eyes now dry. “Do you have a small container of some sort? A jar, maybe?”

Allen said, “Mary Lee…”

She didn’t even glance his way. “Shut *up*, Allen. Do *not* speak to me.”

I said, “I’ll find something.”

“Thank you.”

She walked to the garage with me, but refused my offer for her to come in. I went inside, found a bottle of vitamins—Meredith’s, I supposed—which was nearly empty, and dumped the few remaining capsules into a bowl. I took two bottles of cold water from the fridge and carried them and the empty vitamin bottle back outside. “Here you go, ma’am.”

“Thank you.” Mary Lee had composed herself; she accepted the items with quiet dignity. “You’re a very kind young man.”

I said, “I’m terribly sorry for your loss.”

She gazed up at me. “Do you have children?”

“No, ma’am. We have nieces and nephews. But I know it’s not the same.”

Her gaze never wavered. “He was my only child. There is nothing in our faith that can adequately explain this to me. No one can ever make me believe that this was God’s will.”

I said, “No, ma’am. That’s one reason why I’m not a man of faith.”

She nodded. “Thank you for the water.”

“You’re welcome.”

I went back to the porch and resumed sweeping, as I watched Mary Lee walk back to the curb and scrape some soil into the vitamin bottle. Saving some of the earth from where her son had last lain.

Allen was still standing where I’d left him, hands hanging at his sides, staring into the distance.

Mary Lee screwed the top onto the bottle then sat back down on the street.

They still hadn't moved by the time I was done sweeping and took the broom inside. I lowered the garage door and went to find Pete.

He'd moved to the back patio, textbook in his lap. "What've you been doing?"

"Trying not to punch Jacob Baldwin's father in the face."

He froze, staring at me. "He's out there? Right now?"

"Him and Mom both."

"Did you talk to them?"

"Yup. They sent Jacob to gay conversion camp."

He sucked in a breath. "Holy *shit*. They *told* you that?"

"Mr. Baldwin saw my wedding ring. He assumed I was simpatico."

"What did you *say?*"

"I informed them that conversion therapy is illegal in New Mexico."

"Only for minors."

"I left that part out. They spent eighty thousand dollars to send him here."

"*Eighty thousand??* What the fucking *fuck??*"

"They re-mortgaged their house."

"*Jesus*." Pete turned his highlighter in his fingers. "That's far more expensive than is typical."

"Yeah? How much is typical?"

"Ten to twenty thousand. Still absurdly expensive, but nowhere near what these people paid."

"Depending on the size of this camp, someone's making a shit-ton of money."

Pete crossed his arms, frowning. "Maybe that's the point."

"Conversion therapy as a get rich quick scheme? That's *nuts*."

"Not if it works. Did you call Brian?"

"No. I'll do that now."

Brian didn't answer. I left a voicemail, telling him that I'd met Jacob's parents, but not repeating the conversation.

A couple of hours later, Pete and I were on the front porch. There was no sign of the Baldwins. Kevin and Kristen pulled into the driveway and climbed out of the car, carrying two pizzas. Kristen said, "We come bearing gifts."

I said, "Yum. I'll get plates and napkins."

As we ate, I filled them in on my conversation with the Baldwins. Kristen was horrified. "How can any parent send their kid away to be abused like that?"

I said, "I'd hope that they didn't realize what the treatment would entail."

Kevin said, "Sure. You'd expect counseling. Maybe chopping wood and other manly pursuits. Not rape and beatings."

Pete wiped grease from his fingers. "There have been conversion therapies used that were more aversive. Shock treatment while watching gay porn. That sort of thing."

Kristen said, "This camp must be run by a sadist."

My phone rang; Brian Cochrane's name appeared on the caller ID. I answered, "Hey, Brian. You got my message?"

"I did. Are you home?"

"We're on the front porch. Come on over."

He arrived twenty minutes later and dragged a chair from the opposite end of the porch to join us. "So. The Baldwins."

I said, "They sent Jacob to a gay conversion camp."

Brian's jaw dropped. "No *shit*. They didn't tell me *that*."

Kevin asked, "What did they tell you?"

"That it was a church camp." Brian's expression darkened. "They *lied* to me."

Pete said, "I'm sure there was a religious component to the conversion therapy. There almost always is. They probably figured they weren't technically lying to you."

Brian said to me, "But they told you."

"Mr. Baldwin thought he was talking to a like-minded married man." I repeated the rest of the conversation to Brian.

"*Eighty thousand dollars??*"

"Yep. Fifty up front and five a week. Jacob had been there for six weeks."

Brian shook his head. "No wonder he was in such terrible shape. Pete, what generally goes on at these camps?"

"Counseling, usually Christian-based. Sometimes religious training. Often, rugged outdoor activities. Sometimes, aversion therapy."

"What kind of aversion?"

"Electric shock has been used."

Brian asked, "Has rape been used?"

"I've never heard of that."

I said, "It makes sense though, in a sadistic setting. Discouraging kids from having sex by subjecting them to the worst sex possible."

Kristen was shaking her head, her eyes closed. "Those poor kids."

Kevin asked, "Did the Baldwins give you any indication of where the camp was?"

Brian said, "No. They put Jacob on a plane in Indianapolis, bound for Dallas then Lubbock. They were bewildered that he'd ended up in New Mexico."

I said, "You're still going to interview the survivor in Montana this weekend?"

"Yeah." Brian sighed. "Maybe he can give me a better indication of where he was."

Pete said, "It must be up Route 506 somewhere."

Brian said, "Sure. But there are dozens of secondary roads that turn off 506 and lead nowhere. We've had the chopper up looking but haven't found anything so far. There's too much wilderness to cover. We searched for a GPS signal from Jacob's phone, but nothing pinged."

I said, "Travis hadn't heard from Jacob for six weeks. His phone's battery is probably long dead."

Kristen shuddered. "It is *horrifying* to think that there are kids still out there, suffering through what Jacob did."

Brian's expression was grim. "I need to go. Got an early flight to Billings in the morning."

Kevin said, "Good luck."

"Thanks. I expect I'll need it."

Chapter 14

Saturday, June 15

On Saturday we'd planned a hike, an all-day trek through Dog Canyon. The round trip was approximately 13 miles and rose more than 3000 feet in elevation. Leashed dogs were welcome, but we were afraid that the ground would be too hot for Ammo's paws.

Steve drove; we all piled into his extended-cab pickup truck and drove to Oliver Lee State Park, where we paid our $5.00 fee and struck out on the trail.

The weather was perfect, and the views were gorgeous. I snapped photos along the way to send to my family. Pete and Steve were walking together ahead of Kevin, Kristen, Meredith and me, talking non-stop about their plans for everything they wanted to do once we moved here permanently.

Meredith leaned toward me and lowered her voice, gesturing with her head at Pete and Steve. "Isn't it great? Steve has been *so* excited to have Pete here."

"It is. Pete's been impatiently waiting all spring to get here. They FaceTime every week, but it's not the same."

"No." Meredith smiled. "It's wonderful to see them both so happy."

"Can't argue with that." And I wouldn't argue. My concerns about Alamogordo's homophobia paled—somewhat—in the light of Pete's obvious joy.

Until we got home.

We'd been gone for more than ten hours. Steve was staying for dinner; Pete and Meredith were going to throw together a meal of tortillas and refried beans. As Steve pulled into the driveway, Kristen said, "What's that in the front yard?"

We climbed out of the truck and walked back down the driveway. In our front yard, centered on the house but at the edge of the street, were three white crosses.

The outer two came to just above my knees; the center one reached my waist. Each of them was labeled on the crossbar with a different Bible verse. *Genesis 19* on the left. *Leviticus 18:22* in the center. *Romans 1:26-27* on the right.

We all stared at the display for a second. Steve spat, "Those *fuckers*," as Kristen said, "What the holy *fuck?*"

Kevin squatted down to examine the crosses more closely without touching them. "Jamie? Take pictures of those, please?"

I did, capturing closeups of each cross then several shots of the entire scene, as Meredith called 911. She hung up after a conversation with the dispatcher, and we waited.

The shock was wearing off, and I was getting mad. "They did this in broad daylight! *No one* saw them?"

Kevin said, "Someone may have and didn't think it was unusual. Especially if they were at a distance."

Steve said, "*Everyone's* at a distance. You guys are kinda isolated here."

We weren't, really. We could see several houses from our own. But I had to admit, if I spotted someone in one of the neighbors' yards from where I was standing, I wouldn't be able to tell what he, she, or they were doing.

We waited for a few more minutes. Finally, a patrol car turned onto the street. I didn't recognize the officer who climbed out—the first female APD officer I'd seen.

She shook her head when she saw the crosses and turned to Pete. "Officer Garza. Are you Mr. Ferguson?"

"Yes, ma'am."

Garza nodded to Meredith. "Ms. Lagai. You live at this address, right?"

Meredith said, "That's right."

"Okay." Garza began to take her own photos, circling the crosses, documenting the scene more thoroughly than I had. "You just found this?"

I said, "Yes, ma'am. We just got home from hiking Dog Canyon."

"Any idea who might be responsible?"

"No, ma'am."

"And you had an incident earlier in the week, right? A note was left?"

I said, "Yes, ma'am. Detective Reed found fingerprints on the note, but they weren't in the system."

"Yes. I heard." Garza shook her head again. "Let me get these into evidence."

She gloved, opened the trunk of the cruiser, and produced three large paper sacks. She labeled each then tugged each cross out of the ground—they weren't hammered in deeply—and inserted it into the appropriate sack. "Okay, I'll send these to forensics. If we get prints, we'll see if they match the ones on your note." She examined Kevin over the top of her sunglasses. "Do I know you?"

Kevin sighed. "Do you watch *Two Days to Solve?*"

Recognition dawned on Garza's face. "Riiiight. LAPD. Are you visiting?"

"Yes, ma'am. I'm Jamie's brother."

"Ah. Okay." Garza nodded to us. "I'll be in touch, and I'll drive down this street whenever I get a chance. You all watch your backs."

I said, "Yes, ma'am."

We went inside, locking the doors behind us. Kristen went out back with Ammo; Kevin and Meredith were talking to Steve about what the police would probably do next.

Pete began removing dinner ingredients from the fridge. He was outwardly calm, placing items one by one on the countertop, but he'd said almost nothing since we'd discovered the crosses. I edged close to him. "Pete?"

"I'm thinking."

"Okay." I'd leave him to it. Maybe this was the jolt he needed to snap out of his denial.

Kristen brought Ammo in, and we told her what Officer Garza had said. She perched on a barstool, shaking her head. "There's not much the cops can do yet, is there?"

Kevin said, "Not unless they get a tip from someone."

The scent of refried beans was beginning to emanate from the stove, making my stomach rumble. Steve and Meredith joined Pete at the counter while Kevin, Kristen and I retreated to the back porch with beer.

I said, “I’ve never faced anything like this before. I’ve been called names...but nothing like this.”

Kevin said quietly, with an eye on the door, “You sure you want to live here?”

“This morning I was feeling better about it.” I studied the depths of my beer bottle. “Pete’s so happy here.”

“Gotta think about yourself too.”

“I’m not a quitter.”

Kristen said, “No. But if you’re facing a rattlesnake, you back away slowly. That’s not quitting, that’s self-preservation.”

I sighed. “Maybe it’s just a gopher snake with delusions of grandeur.”

Kevin chuckled. But I didn’t feel like laughing.

Chapter 15

Sunday, June 16

After lunch on Sunday, Steve and Meredith went to Steve's for the afternoon. Kevin and Kristen loaded their luggage into the rental; we hugged goodbye in the driveway. Kevin spoke softly into my ear. "Watch your six."

"Roger that."

He stepped back and regarded me solemnly. "You may have poked a hornet's nest."

"I know. We'll be careful. Please don't mention any of this to Dad."

"Oh, hell, no." Kevin slugged me in the shoulder. "Love you, short stuff."

"*Ow*. Love you too. I think."

He grinned and climbed into the driver's seat. Kristen waved as they pulled away, and Pete and I were alone.

I turned to him. "What are your plans for the rest of the day?"

"I thought I'd build that bookshelf." Pete was gazing down the street, a slight frown on his face. "I need to hammer."

"Need help?"

"No." He glanced at me. "What are you gonna do?"

"I believe that I will sit on the front porch and read."

"You mean watch for anyone who might drive down our street."

"That, too."

He seemed to be considering a comment, then decided against it. "Okay."

I followed him into the house, lowering the garage door behind us. I got a Coke from the fridge, noting a row of clean jelly jars in the dish drainer that hadn't been there before. "What's planned for those jars?"

Pete gave me a look. "They're for the soil from under Jacob's body. For Ammo's training when we get back to Santa Monica."

That stopped me. "Oh. That's… Do you really want to do that? Carry Jacob home with us?"

"It's not Jacob. It's just chemicals."

"Tell his mother that. She took soil home with her, too."

He regarded me, frowning. "You're not the sentimental type. What's going on with you?"

I strode past him, to the doors that led to the patio, then turned and jerked my thumb over my shoulder. "I cannot stop thinking about the fact that there is a *goddamn conversion camp,* somewhere in those mountains, that tortured that sweet kid. I cannot stop wishing that I had told his father exactly what I thought about him and his version of Christianity. And I cannot stop thinking about the other kids at that camp and what they're going through."

He winced. "I can't stop thinking about them, either. I feel helpless, too. But how is training Ammo on the spot across the street any different from training him on the same soil in a jar, somewhere else?"

"It's not." I took in a deep breath then blew it out. "Of course, we should take some dirt home. It's the reasonable thing to do. It's just that I'm holding onto all this anger with no place to dump it. Reason is struggling to be heard through the anger."

The corner of his mouth tipped up. "That's very insightful."

"Thank you."

"Do you want to hammer?"

"No. I want to find the people who are hammering crosses into our yard and beat them senseless."

"If we catch one in the act, I won't stop you. Until then, maybe you should burn off some anger with exercise."

"I will." I was feeling a bit calmer already…calm enough to get out of my own head. "You don't seem angry. What's going on with *you?*"

He gazed past me, out the back door. "I am angry, but… You and I do anger differently. Yours burns hot and fast. Mine simmers and then usually morphs into something else. Right now, what I mostly feel is helpless paralysis." He lifted his hands then dropped them to his sides. "I need to build this bookcase. To see a tangible result from my efforts, and to remind myself that I'm not helpless within my own circle of control."

I went to him and took his chin between my thumb and forefinger, tipping it down slightly so that our eyes met. "We are not helpless. We are rich and powerful, and *we will prevail*. Eventually."

He kissed my fingers. "It's the *eventually* part that drives you crazy."

I took a step back and raised my fist in the air. "What do we want? *Justice!* When do we want it? *Now!*"

He chuckled. "Lord, give me patience. *Now*."

"Yeah, yeah." I kissed him. "Go build your bookcase."

I helped Pete haul the boards that Kevin and I had stained to the basement. I left Ammo with him, then tied on my running shoes and went to the back yard. I mentally sketched a running path, along the wall and weaving in and out of the trees, then took off and ran hard for thirty minutes.

It worked. Afterwards, I felt considerably less angry. More purposeful. I chose a book from our office and removed Pete's shotgun from its locked cabinet. I loaded the gun then went to the porch, propped the gun against the wall beside me, and began to read.

I wasn't really expecting to see anyone that afternoon. For the first 45 minutes, all was quiet. Occasionally a car would appear on Las Lomas. Once, a pair of F-16s zoomed overhead, leaving Holloman AFB.

I was absorbed in my book when I heard an engine approaching. I lifted my head to watch. A car circled the end of the cul-de-sac and stopped at our mailbox. The driver, a woman, squinted at me, then cut the engine and got out. Rather than approach the house, though, she opened the door to the back seat. For a moment I couldn't see why, then she came around the front of the car with a leashed German shepherd.

I waited. The woman stopped at the end of our driveway and waved. "Hello! I'm Cora Valdez, from Alamogordo Search and Rescue."

Aha. I left the shotgun where it was and walked onto the driveway. "Hi, I'm Jamie Brodie. What's your dog's name?"

"Frasier."

I shook hands with Cora then ruffled Frasier's ears. "Is he a specialist?"

"He does live search and rescue, and he's certified for avalanche work. I understand that you have a certified cadaver dog."

"Yes, ma'am. Come on up to the porch."

Cora took a seat. "Whew! It's a hot one."

"Can I get you something to drink?"

"No, no, I'm fine." She smiled at me. "How long has your dog been certified?"

"Just under a year. He was a Marine bomb detection dog, but he retired from that."

"No kidding! He must have a great nose."

"He sure does."

She lowered her voice, even though there was no one in sight. "You and your dog found Danny Norman last year, right?"

"Yes, ma'am. Did you know Danny?"

"Not well. But Joey and Patti are regular donors to the search and rescue group. They're fine people."

I nodded. "We met them in December."

Cora frowned slightly, then gave her head a slight shake. "Anyway, I just wanted to stop by and introduce myself. Dr. Smith is our veterinarian, too, and he told me you all were here for the summer."

"Only half the summer, really. But if you need our services while we're here, let us know."

"What's your dog's name?"

"Ammo. He's a six-year-old yellow Lab."

She smiled. "Great name. Are you his handler?"

"I'm certified, but my husband is the primary handler. He's a former cop, so our police departments prefer to use him."

"Sure. We don't have much local work. Typically, what happens is that someone goes missing in the desert or mountains." She nodded to the spot across the street. "Like what happened here, I guess."

"Sort of." I didn't want to get into the details of the Baldwin case with her. "Do you want to meet Ammo?"

"I'd love to."

"Be right back." I lifted the shotgun to carry it inside. Cora raised an eyebrow but didn't comment.

I left the shotgun in the kitchen and trotted down the stairs to the basement. Pete had two of the shelves attached to the sides of the bookcase and was measuring. He glanced up. "What?"

"A lady from Alamogordo Search and Rescue is here with her dog. She wants to meet Ammo. She'd probably like to meet you, too."

At the sound of his name, Ammo scrambled to his feet. Pete's expression lightened. "Cool! Come on, Ammo, let's introduce ourselves."

He and Ammo galloped up the stairs and onto the porch. I took a bottle of water from the fridge for Cora and followed. When I got outside, Ammo and Frasier were greeting each other, as were Cora and Pete.

Cora stayed for about a half hour, trading dog training stories with Pete. Finally, she glanced at her watch. "I should go. Our next business meeting is the first Tuesday in July. If you're still in town, you're more than welcome to attend. Bring Ammo and meet the rest of the team."

Pete beamed. "Thank you so much. We accept."

After Cora left, all fell quiet again. Pete and Ammo returned to the basement. I replaced the shotgun against the wall and re-absorbed myself in my book.

A couple of hours later, I was just starting to feel hungry when Pete came outside. "All done. It looks good."

"We should choose which books we want to keep down there, since it's our safe room."

"Hm. Have to think about that. You getting hungry yet?"

"You read my mind. Want any help?"

"Nope. I'll heat up leftovers. You stay here." Pete eyed the shotgun. "Ammo, come."

We ate bean and cheese burritos on the porch, accompanied by Dos Equis, chatting about search and rescue. When we finished, Pete carried the plates inside and returned with more beer. He sat down, took a swig, and nodded at the shotgun. "You realize that if anything happens, it'll likely be after dark."

"I know. But why take chances?"

He snorted softly. "Is that a Southern thing? Sitting on your front porch with a shotgun?"

I smiled. "Sort of. I remember Sarge talking about the difference between the Lowcountry South and the Appalachian South. Lowcountry Southerners greet you on their front porch with sweet iced tea, then talk about you behind your back after you leave. Appalachian Southerners greet you on their front porch with a shotgun, but once they accept you as a friend, you have a friend for life."

"But Sarge and your dad are Lowcountry Southerners."

"Yeah, but they were Marines, who are known for saying what they want to say right to your face. And my mom was an Appalachian Southerner." I gestured with my beer bottle in a sweep that took in as much of Alamogordo as we could see. "I'm guessing these people understand shotguns better than sweet tea."

He was quiet for a moment. "I think I just figured something out."

"What?"

"Your experience of small towns is with Southern small towns. Is that what you were expecting to find here?"

"Huh." I considered that. "You could be right."

"Tell me about Southern small towns."

I thought about everything I'd ever heard from my dad's family about growing up in small-town Beaufort, South Carolina.

"There are usually three or four families that have been there for generations, that unofficially run the place. Anyone who moves into town is considered a newcomer, even if they arrived twenty years ago. But, when someone new moves in, everyone in the neighborhood shows up with a casserole. They may only be curious about what you've done to the inside of old man Howard's house, but they know the price of admission is that casserole."

"You'll note that no one has brought us a casserole."

"Yes. Noted. Anyway. The main topic of conversation on the street is always the weather, and you do not pass anyone on the street or in the grocery store without acknowledgement. If it's a stranger, you say 'hey.' If it's someone you know but don't much like, you stop and talk about the weather. If it's someone you know and like, you stop and mention the weather, then ask about their family. There's always one spot in town, maybe a barber shop, where a handful of old men hang out every day and talk politics and the weather."

"You'll note that no one walks here. Even in town. Even on Steve's street, the neighbors are never out walking."

"Yeah. There are nice sidewalks here, but no one uses them. More people walk in LA than here. And here's another difference. In the South, people sit on their front porches. Here, they hang out in their own back yards. Might as well be in Brentwood or Bel Air."

"Remember last winter, when Christine told me I'd moved back to Barstow?"

"Yes."

"She wasn't wrong. But it's not just Barstow and Alamogordo. It's Victorville, and Twentynine Palms, and Rosamond, and even to some extent Lancaster. Small desert towns where nearly everyone is from somewhere else, and the residents with the longest local pedigrees are usually Hispanic. People come to work at the military base. Some stay, most don't. People mind their own business. They don't want to get involved in their neighbors' problems, often because they barely know them."

I frowned at the setting sun. "So you're suggesting that my expectations for Alamogordo were too high."

"In a sense, yes."

"And you didn't think to mention this before we built here?"

"I didn't realize what your expectations would be until today. Maybe it should have occurred to me. It didn't."

"Well. We're here now. We have friends in law enforcement who are working on our behalf. What else should we do?"

"What else *can* we do?"

I shook my head slowly. "Dunno. I'm working on it. Are you mad at Kev and Kristen?"

He sighed deeply. "No."

"I'm glad to hear that."

"I know they're being protective."

"Kevin's been protecting me since we were toddlers. It's a hard habit to break."

"I don't want him to break it." Pete gazed out at the scrub to the west. "I just… It never occurred to me that we might encounter homophobia here. Maybe it should have. But… I had expectations for this small town, too. That people would mind their own damn business. I thought we might be gossiped about behind our backs, but that we'd be left alone to our faces. I'm having trouble wrapping my head around this."

"Understandable. I guess we'll see what happens next."

Pete sagged. "Let's hope *nothing* happens next."

"Yeah." But I didn't think it was over.

The sun had just set when Brian Cochrane drove onto our street. He circled and parked in front of our house. When he stepped from his car I called, "You can park on the driveway, you know."

"I hate to, though. It's so pretty." Our driveway was paved with specially engineered solar panels.

He ruffled Ammo's ears and accepted the offer of a beer. Once he was settled, I said, "How was Montana?"

"Hot." Brian drank greedily then set his bottle aside. "I had to ride out on the range a couple of miles to meet up with our guy."

Pete asked, "What did he tell you?"

"His name is Garrett Cook. He was at the camp just over a year ago."

I said, "His parents sent him?"

"Yes, but he went willingly. He didn't want to be gay. His parents and grandparents together scraped up the fee, which at the time was a flat rate of $40,000."

Pete grunted. "That's still steep, but more in line with others I've heard."

"Anyway, Garrett was only at the camp for two weeks. He said it became clear almost immediately that it wasn't the right place for him. He was expecting counseling. Learning life skills to help him overcome his attraction to men."

I said, "And there wasn't any."

"No. Lots of hard physical work—chopping wood, scrubbing toilets—and preaching, but Garrett never saw a psychologist. He asked about it and was told that he had to be there a month before he qualified to see the counselor."

Pete scowled. "That's not how it works."

"Right, and Garrett knew that. He'd done some research before signing up, and he realized this place wasn't interested in conversion. So he told them that he wanted to leave."

Something in Brian's expression made my guts clench. "And that was a mistake?"

"Yup. To back up a little, he said there were four employees at the camp. Two oversaw work details and logistics, and did the cooking. One, the preacher, was part-time. The fourth one was responsible for the 'therapy.'"

Pete said, "But you said there wasn't therapy."

"There wasn't *counseling*. There *was* aversion therapy. Twice while he was there, Garrett was taken into a room and hooked up to a device that fastened around his dick. Meant to measure arousal, apparently. Then he was shown porn, both straight and gay. If he responded to the gay porn, he received a shock. If he didn't respond to the straight porn, he received a shock."

I squeaked. "In his *dick?*"

"Yeah." Brian grimaced. "He said it wasn't bad, but still… Anyway. When Garrett told the guys he wanted to leave, the two that seemed to be in charge said okay, they'd make the arrangements for the next day. Garrett went back to the dorms, packed his stuff and went to bed. He woke up as he was being dragged from his bed by the 'therapy' guy. Garrett fought, but he's skinny. He said the guy was a beast. His word. He broke his nose, broke his ribs, then kicked him in the head and knocked him out. When Garrett came to, the guy was raping him."

Pete and I spoke in stereo. "*Fuuuuuuck.*"

"Garrett passed out again from the pain. When he came to, the guy was gone."

I said, "You said this was a dorm. No one helped Garrett fight?"

"No. Once he was gone, though, a couple of them helped Garrett clean himself up and get back to bed. The next morning, Garrett dragged his suitcase and himself to the office. The guy who'd raped him wasn't around; the other two never said a word. They marched him about a half mile uphill and over a ridge, where there was a tiny airstrip, and a two-seater Cessna waiting. The pilot flew him to Lubbock and handed him a plane ticket to Billings."

Pete asked, "Could he tell anything about his location?"

"No. They flew east from the camp to Lubbock, but that doesn't help much."

I said, "Is he okay now?"

"Yeah. Once he got to Billings, he called his parents, who took him straight to the hospital. He spent a couple of days there and got fixed up. I asked him why he didn't report anything to the police; he said he'd just wanted to move past it. Besides, he knew the camp wasn't in Montana, and he figured there was nothing the local cops could do." Brian shrugged. "He was probably right."

Pete was frowning as he thought. "You said all three of these cases had a drug in their system."

“Yeah. Garrett said he wasn’t given any pills to take, so they must have added it to food or drink.”

“Did he know any names?”

“No. None of the employees ever used their names.” Brian drained his beer. “Anyway. Now I have descriptions of these people, but that doesn’t help without the location of the camp.”

Pete asked hesitantly, “What’s Garrett’s state of mind now?”

“He went to a counselor who, fortunately, ended up working with him and his parents to accept his orientation. He’s seeing a guy now who works on a neighboring ranch.” Brian slapped his knees and stood. “A tiny bit of happy ending, anyway. I’d better get home. Gotta do laundry before tomorrow.”

I said, “Thanks for stopping by.”

“Sure. I knew you’d want to hear.”

After Brian left, Pete and I sat in silence for a while. The heat of the day dissipated; the light in the west faded until all was dark. The only visible light shone from the houses beyond Las Lomas, and the establishments along White Sands Blvd. in the distance. Eventually, Pete spoke. “What’s on your schedule for tomorrow?”

“We need groceries.”

“Okay. Then we could visit Mandy’s GSA together.”

I said, “Sounds like a plan.”

Chapter 16

Monday, June 17

On Monday morning we composed a grocery list as we ate breakfast—Kevin and Kristen's visit had depleted our supplies—then headed to the store. Pete seemed to be restored to his normal self, chatting as we cruised the aisles about the items that we had to buy now but would be able to make or grow ourselves when we lived here full time.

He was engrossed in squeezing melons; I was leaning on the cart handle, people-watching, when I spotted a familiar face.

The chihuahua owner from the veterinarian's office.

She hadn't seen us yet; she was scanning shelves as she pushed her cart, looking for something. I straightened up, crossed my arms, and plastered a grin on my face.

My movement must have caught her eye. She glanced my way then did a double take, her mouth hanging open.

I said, "Well, hey, there. I remember you from Dr. Smith's office."

That got Pete's attention. He turned, a cantaloupe in each hand. I watched as the woman mentally debated what to do. Confront or flee? Her cheeks flamed, and she gripped the handle of her cart so tightly that her knuckles turned white. "Yes. I remember you. And your kind is not welcome here."

I said, "Our kind? You mean… people from…" I gasped. "*...California?*"

Pete snorted softly. The woman hissed, "You *know* what I mean."

I shook my head sadly. "Pete, I'm crushed. She doesn't like us because we're *queer*."

The woman's eyes widened at my word choice. Pete said, "That's not very hospitable."

"Nope." I lowered my voice. "I'd expect better from an animal lover, but no. You're just a common bigot." I leaned in closer; the woman drew her head and shoulders back. "We *know* how to handle bigots. The police have taken fingerprints from every single piece of evidence that's been left on our property. As soon as they ID whoever it is, that person or those people are *going to jail*. Because we will press charges from here to Albuquerque. You tell everyone you know… *you have messed with the wrong queers*. And we intend to make you *extremely* sorry."

The woman's red face blanched. She spun her cart in a 180 and scurried away from us. I called after her, "Have a blessed day."

Pete watched her go, then turned to me. "So we've completely given up on winning over the locals?"

"Pfft. Do you *want* to win her and her ilk over? I don't. I want to make them *pariahs*. I want *them* to consider leaving town. I want…"

He held up his hand. "Got it."

"Seriously, Pete. Do you think that everyone in town will gradually come around? Will eventually accept us with open arms?"

"No. But I *wish* they would. And you hope they *don't*."

"That's not true. It's not a matter of *hoping* for anything. It's a matter of *seeing* these people for who they are and *always will be*. They've *clearly* demonstrated their character and intentions. Now it's our turn to show them who *we* are. And *always will be*."

He sighed deeply. "God, I'm tired of this."

"Of what? Standing up for ourselves?"

"Of *having* to stand up for ourselves." He gave me a wry sideways look. "Or, more accurately, of *you* having to stand up for us."

Hm. There was plenty to unpack there, but I wasn't inclined to open that conversation in a grocery store. I said, "How'm I doing so far?"

He just shook his head.

The GSA at NMSU-Alamogordo met in a tiny lounge belonging to the Social Sciences department. It was a cramped room with battered, mismatching chairs and a coffee pot that had seen better days. A bulletin board on one wall was pinned with flyers for events that had already happened.

Mandy McCarthy was already there, arranging a couple dozen homemade chocolate chip cookies on a plate. She hugged us both. "Welcome! I'm so glad you could come."

I said, "We're delighted to help out. Where are the students?"

"They'll be here in a few minutes. The last class of the day just ended."

We both accepted a cookie and chatted with Mandy about trivial things for a moment, until the students began to file in. There were eight. Two of them said hello to us, three smiled shyly in our direction, and the other three gave us sideways glances. All but one took fistfuls of cookies and dragged chairs into a circle.

Pete and I joined them. One girl—the one without cookies—said, "Hi, Dr. Ferguson, it's great to see you again."

"You too, Alicia."

Mandy sat beside me. "You all remember Dr. Ferguson from last week, and this is his husband, Dr. Jamie Brodie."

I said, "*Please* call me Jamie."

A couple of them chuckled. One of the girls asked, "What kind of doctor?"

"Ph.D. In history. But I'm a librarian at UCLA."

Mandy said, "How long have you two been married now?"

Pete said, "Almost four years. Our anniversary is in a couple of weeks."

One of the boys, his face almost hidden under a curtain of hair, asked, "Do you get hassled?"

I said, "At home, almost never. But we live in one of the most progressive cities in one of the most progressive states in the country. It's totally different than here."

A couple of the kids sighed wistfully. Another boy started to ask something when the door opened, and another kid entered. Mandy said, "Hi, Dylan, I didn't think you'd be here."

"I was able to change my plans." Dylan took one cookie and sat.

The boy that had been about to speak previously asked, "Do you get hassled here?"

Pete and I glanced at each other. I said, "Yeah. We've had a couple of threats."

Dylan said, "From people in my mother's church."

Oho. We had a group of suspects. I asked, "Which church?"

"The Holiness church up at the corner of Scenic and Indian Wells Road."

Pete asked, "Do you know for sure that the threats are coming from them?"

"I think so. I don't know exactly who, but I know they've talked about you at Wednesday prayer meeting. They're praying for God to remove you from Alamogordo."

I said, "Gee. How I'll hate to disappoint them."

They all laughed. One of the girls said, "Good for you."

Pete said, "I'm an ex-cop. Jamie was raised by Marines. We won't run."

The kids all murmured encouragement.

The students kept asking questions and we discussed the daily challenges of living as a gay married couple, which Pete and I assured them weren't that different from the challenges of living as any married couple. Then one boy who hadn't spoken before said, "There are lots of homeless and runaway gay kids in LA, aren't there?"

Pete said, "That's right."

"What are you two doing to help them?"

I decided to let Pete handle the question. He said, "We donate monthly to the Los Angeles LGBT Center. They're the primary organization in LA that helps homeless queer people. We haven't physically volunteered yet, but that's something I'd like to do."

I asked the kid, "Is that a problem here in Alamogordo?"

He shrugged. "We have homeless people. But who'd run away to *this* place?"

One of the girls said, "I heard there was a camp for runaway gay kids up in the mountains somewhere."

Camp. The hair stood on the back of my neck. I asked, "Where'd you hear about that?"

"My brother goes to NMSU, the main campus, and one of his friends was talking about it. His friend is from Albuquerque, and he knew someone who knew someone who'd been kicked out of his house when he came out to his parents. The guy spent some time at a camp for runaways up in the mountains." She shrugged. "My brother's friend said it was near here, but he had no idea where."

So the word wasn't out that the camp was used for conversion therapy. I said, "Have any of the rest of you heard rumors about a camp in the mountains?"

Most of them shook their heads. Then Dylan said, "I have. But what I heard about wasn't a camp for runaways."

Mandy asked, "What was it for?"

"It's a church camp. At least that's what I heard."

I thought Dylan was hedging and wondered if he'd talk to us after the meeting. One of the girls said, "A church camp for queer kids? Seriously?"

Dylan said, "No, it's not for queer kids. At least not from what I heard."

I asked, "Where is it?"

He shrugged. "I can't ask questions about it. I wasn't supposed to overhear the conversation that I heard."

Mandy glanced at the clock. "We're about out of time. Those of you who are going to pick up trash along the highway on Sunday morning, meet me in the parking lot here at 8:00 in the morning. We'll carpool."

The meeting broke up, and the kids gradually filtered out, until Pete, Mandy and I were left with Dylan. I said, "Dylan, you heard this rumor at church, I'm guessing."

"Not at church, at home. My mom mentioned it to my dad."

"What did she say?"

"That a friend of hers at church said there was a youth camp for future pastors up in the mountains, and she wanted to donate money to it."

Pete asked, "Is that exactly what she said? A youth camp for future pastors?"

"Yeah." Dylan screwed up his face. "She and my dad argued about it. He doesn't go to church, and he didn't want her to give them anything. He's been unemployed for a while. It's not like we have money to spare."

I said, "Dylan, could you do us a favor? If you hear anything else about this camp, could you let Ms. McCarthy know? Then she'll pass the message to us."

Dylan shrugged. "Sure. I might not, though."

"That's fine. Don't ask any questions that are going to create trouble for yourself. Just keep your ears open."

"I can do that."

Pete said, "I suppose you're not out to your parents?"

Dylan wrinkled his nose. "My dad knows. I didn't tell him, he just guessed somehow. He said he didn't care what I did as long as he never heard about it."

Pete was in semi-counseling mode. "Does it bother you? That he's not more supportive?"

"Nah. I'm just happy that he hasn't thrown me out. He doesn't ask, I don't tell. Works for me."

I said, "There's not much gay social life here."

Dylan snorted. "There's *no* gay social life. Which is why I take one class every semester at the NMSU main campus in Las Cruces." He smiled. "I have a boyfriend there. I tell my parents that I need to spend the weekends in Las Cruces so I can use the main campus library. I reckon my dad knows what's up, but like I said, he doesn't ask."

Pete said, "Your mom doesn't suspect?"

"My mom is not the sharpest tool in the shed." Dylan rolled his eyes. "And she's gullible as hell. Believes anything anyone tells her. Including me, fortunately."

"How much longer will you be at NMSU-A?"

"I have two more classes, in the fall. I'll take two classes at the main campus, too." He smirked. "More time in Las Cruces."

I said, "Sounds like a plan."

Chapter 17

Tuesday, June 18

We spent Tuesday morning with Ammo, in the scrub south of our house, training on the scent from Jacob Baldwin's body in the soil that Pete had collected. I wore gloves to diminish the strength of my own scent on the jars we used as sample and decoys. Ammo performed like a champ, locating the scent jar every time.

We spent Tuesday afternoon discussing plans for the basement living space. Pete worked in the garden; I read on the front porch, shotgun at my side. It was a pleasantly mundane day. But it wasn't meant to last.

It was close to bedtime. I was making my final rounds, ensuring that the house was locked and secured, when I noticed that the front porch light was out.

That was odd. The bulb was new; it shouldn't have burned out yet. Suspicious after the events of the past two weeks, I cracked two slats of the plantation blinds in a front window and peered out.

I couldn't see much, but I thought I detected movement. In front of the porch, to the right of the door.

I hurried to the kitchen, where Meredith was packing her lunch for the next day and Pete was rearranging the pantry. "I think there's someone messing around in the front yard."

Meredith dropped her knife. "What?"

"The porch light is out. It shouldn't be. And I thought I saw someone moving."

Pete growled. "Goddamnit. Where'd you leave the shotgun?"

"In the bedroom."

He disappeared then was back in two seconds, carrying the gun. "Meredith, you might need to call 911."

Her eyes were wide. "Okay."

Fortunately, the locks and latches on our front door were well oiled. They slid open silently. Pete eased out onto the porch. I followed, right on his heels.

The bulb from the porch light was lying on the nearest table. Over Pete's shoulder, I saw a shadowy figure—my impression was male—standing in the right-side cactus bed, swinging his arm up and down. Whatever tool he was wielding made a soft *thwack* sound.

Pete racked the shotgun. "Hey!"

The guy jumped like a startled rabbit and fled. I took off after him. Fortunately, he ran like a cartoon character, lots of flailing but little forward motion. I caught him easily in the street and brought him down with a flying tackle, hitting him around the waist—rather than the knees—to cushion my own landing with his flabby body.

I mostly succeeded. Pete charged up behind us. I scrambled to my feet as Pete shoved the shotgun into the back of the guy's neck and yelled, "Stay down! Hands on the back of your head!"

The guy complied, babbling something that I didn't entirely get. "Not my idea" was part of the stream of consciousness.

Pete said, "Shut up."

The guy shut up.

Meredith must have called 911; blue lights turned onto our street and stopped several yards away, headlights and spotlight blinding us. A voice called out, "Lay down the shotgun."

Pete did as instructed. He and I both put our hands up. The guy on the ground started to get up and the cop said, "Don't move."

The guy stayed where he was but started pleading his case. "He was gonna shoot me, officer! I feared for my life!"

The cop quoted Pete. "Shut up."

As he approached, I saw that he was Officer Smallwood, one of the responders when we'd found Jacob Baldwin's body across the street. I said, "Evening, Officer Smallwood."

Smallwood gave me a look but holstered his gun. "Mr. Brodie. What's going on?"

I recounted the events of the previous few minutes. Smallwood nodded. He cuffed the guy and hauled him to his feet. "Otto Pringle. Why am I not surprised?"

Pringle started to whine. "I feared for my life! He was gonna shoot me!"

"No, he wasn't."

"But…"

Smallwood said tiredly, "Otto? Shut up." He deposited Pringle in the back of his cruiser, then returned to us. "Do you want to press charges?"

Pete asked, "Who is he?"

"Otto Pringle. Chronically unemployed, occasional drunk and disorderly."

I said, "Hell, yes, I want to press charges. These people need to stop fucking with us."

Smallwood said, "Let's see what he did."

The police cruiser and Smallwood's flashlight illuminated our front yard. Pringle had ruined two of our cacti, chopping them to bits with a machete, which was still lying by the shreds of plant.

Smallwood snapped on gloves and handled the machete as evidence. "He'll only be fined."

I said, "I don't care. I want an arrest on his record."

Pete asked, "Would his arrest harm anyone else? Children?"

Smallwood said, "Nah. Otto's kids are grown and gone, and his wife left him years ago. The DA might drop the charges if he informs us who put him up to this."

I said, "That would be acceptable. Although I already have an opinion about that."

Smallwood raised an eyebrow at me, a faint grin on his face. "Who's your suspect?"

"Someone from the Holiness Church on Indian Wells." I told Smallwood about our conversation with Dylan.

"Ah." Smallwood didn't seem surprised. "We'll keep that in mind."

Pete asked, "Who's we?"

Smallwood said, "Pretty sure Tobias Reed is the detective on call tonight." He lowered his voice. "Ms. Lagai is highly respected by the Alamogordo PD. We'll make sure this is handled right."

I said, "We appreciate that."

Smallwood nodded sharply. "Not a problem. You all get some rest."

We watched as Smallwood drove away with Pringle, then returned to the house. Pete stuck his head in the door. "Meredith? All clear."

Meredith came to the door. "What happened?"

Pete explained as I screwed the bulb back into the porch light, immediately illuminating the porch and yard. Meredith sorrowfully regarded the remains of the cacti. "Well, shit. And they were just about to bloom."

I said, "We'll replace them tomorrow. Have you heard of Otto Pringle?"

"Unfortunately, yes. He's instigated bar fights with a couple of my clients."

Pete asked, "Would he dream up the idea to destroy our cacti on his own?"

"Nope. Someone put him up to it. But I expect that he'll roll over on whoever it was, if it lets him out of jail sooner. He hates jail."

I said, "He can't drink there."

Meredith snorted. "Exactly."

Chapter 18

Wednesday, June 19

Neither Pete nor I slept well that night. One of us would drift off, then the other would toss and turn and then we'd both be awake again. Finally, at about 3:30, Pete got up and left the room. A half hour later, I finally fell asleep.

I didn't wake up until 9:15. I found Pete fully dressed, at his desk in the office, typing on his laptop. "Whatcha doing?"

"Blogging." He smiled up at me; it was a tired smile. "Did you finally get to sleep?"

"Yeah. Did you sleep somewhere else?"

"No." He frowned at his screen. "I cleaned and reloaded the Glock and the shotgun."

"Ah." Perhaps he was coming to grips with the seriousness of our situation. "Are we going to the garden center this morning?"

"Sure. Do you want a cooked breakfast?"

"Nah. I'll eat cereal. Did you take pictures of the damage?"

"No."

In the morning light, I saw that two more cacti had suffered deep gouges that would likely
prove to be mortal wounds. The remnants of the destroyed plants were beginning to turn brown and curl up. It was depressing. I documented every inch of it, then went inside to eat.

The nursery we used was to the northwest of town. The proprietors, Ross and Dianne Harris, had worked with our builder to landscape our property, and were always friendly.

Today was no exception. This early, we were the only customers. Dianne was at the counter when we walked into the building; she beamed. "Hi, guys!"

Pete said, "Hey, Dianne, how are you?"

"Doin' great. What's new?"

I said, "We need four replacement prickly pear cacti."

She frowned. "Oh? Did some of yours die?"

"Yeah, but they had help." I told her what had happened.

Her jaw dropped. "*No*. Otto *Pringle?*"

Pete asked, "Does that surprise you?"

"It only surprises me that he'd leave his barstool long enough to bother. And Otto's a sloppy drunk, but he isn't generally a malicious type. Someone must have paid him."

I said, "Any idea who that someone might be?"

"No… but I'll keep my ears open, for sure."

Pete said, "We appreciate that."

She nodded briskly. "Well. Let's get you some new prickly pear."

We followed Dianne out to the nursery, where we chose four healthy young prickly pear plants. Ross joined us; when he heard why we were there, he said, "We won't charge you for these."

I said, "No, no. You can't just give us four more healthy plants."

"Sure I can."

"No, you can't."

Pete said, "Ross, you won't win an argument with him."

Dianne chuckled. Ross said, "Okay, then, you pay for them, but we'll come plant 'em for you."

I said, "Seriously, you don't need to do that."

Ross crossed his arms. "Think of it this way. Someone in town is hassling you, right? Let's show 'em that you have support from the business community here. Besides, Alex and Connor need something to do besides play video games today."

Alex and Connor were Ross and Dianne's teenage sons. Pete and I conferred with a look; he said, "It's a deal."

"All right." Ross shook our hands. "We'll be out in an hour or so."

"Perfect."

We paid Dianne for the cacti and went back to town. I said, "Should we stop for lunch somewhere?"

Pete shot me a look. "You're wanting to show your face in town?"

"Yes, I am."

We stopped at our favorite Mexican restaurant on White Sands Boulevard. Fortunately, we were well ahead of the lunch rush. We were seated and had ordered when we saw Brian Cochrane come in, accompanied by a guy we recognized as another state trooper.

We waved them over to join us. Brian introduced his companion as the captain of the Alamogordo detachment, Grady Carpenter. We shook hands with Carpenter, who said, "We hear you fellas had some trouble last night. Saw it on the report this morning."

Pete said, "Yup. You all know anything about Otto Pringle?"

Brian said, "He's a local nuisance. We've never dealt with him, but I know he's a constant thorn in APD's side."

I said, "Thorn. Cactus. Ha ha."

Carpenter snorted. Brian smirked. "Yeah, sorry about that. Anyway, I'm glad we ran into you. We got the lab reports from those other cases that matched Jacob Baldwin's."

"And?"

"They all had the same drug in their blood. It's still not identified, but at least now we know that the cases are likely to be all connected."

Pete asked, "Jacob's tox results matched, too?"

"Yes. We were able to get a bit more information about the other two cases, the ones that were minors and wouldn't talk to me. Like Garrett, our Montana case, the others didn't know they'd been drugged. Unlike Garrett, they had no idea where they were. Their parents thought they were in Texas."

I said, "Like the Baldwins."

"Exactly."

We got home just as Ross and his sons arrived. An hour later, our new cacti were in place. I handed Ross, Alex, and Connor bottles of water from the fridge. "There you go, Northern California spring water. The best there is."

Ross said, "Thanks. You'll want to water the cacti, too."

"I will." I waved goodbye to the Harrises, then watered the plants with the buckets from our morning showers. "Welcome to your new home, prickly pears."

The cacti didn't answer, but they seemed happy.

Back in the house, it was cool and quiet. I found Pete asleep in the family room, one hand dangling off the sofa, his criminal justice textbook open on his chest. Ammo was napping too; he lifted his head and gave me a quizzical look.

I whispered, "Ammo, stay," and slipped out of the room. I got a Coke from the fridge, went to the back porch, and called Kevin.

He answered immediately. "Hey, has something else happened?"

"Well, hello to you, too. Yes, something else has happened."

He drew in a breath. "I knew it. What?"

I told him about our cactoid adventures. "Pure nuisance harassment. Nothing more."

"I don't know about that. They've escalated to destruction of property."

"Yes, but it was low level. They could have spray painted the house and driveway, but they didn't."

"They still might."

I sighed. "The cops are working on it. What else can we do?"

Kevin was quiet for a moment. "I don't like it."

"Neither do I. I'm open to suggestion."

"How is Pete handling it?"

"He cleaned and reloaded both guns last night. Although…" I'd forgotten about our conversation in the grocery store. "He said something odd the other day. That he was tired of me having to stand up for us all the time. Like… he's shirking his duties in that area or something."

"In what context?"

I told him about the lady from the vet's office. Kevin asked, "Do you think he's not carrying his weight in defending the two of you?"

"I *don't* think that. It hadn't occurred to me. Let's face it, I'm just better at calling people on their bullshit than he is."

He barked a laugh. "*That's* true. You think your cactus chopper was related to this church the kid mentioned at your meeting?"

"Probably. It's the same sort of one-degree-removed semi-harmless fuckery that whoever it is has been orchestrating."

"Watch your back and don't go anywhere alone."

"Done and done."

Pete wandered onto the patio, stretching and yawning. I said, "Pete's up from his nap. I'll talk to you later."

"Okay. *Be careful.*"

"We will." I said goodbye.

Pete dropped to the seat beside me. "Who was that?"

"Kevin. Good nap?"

"Yeah. Kinda groggy now, though. What did Kev say?"

"Nothing useful. I told him we were waiting for the cops to do their jobs."

"Mm hm." He rubbed his eyes. "Ugh. I had a list of stuff to do today."

"You needed sleep more. Tomorrow's a new day."

He snorted. "Right, Little Orphan Annie. I'm gonna call Meredith and see what she wants to do about dinner."

"Okie dokie."

He went inside. I gazed at the mountains and pondered. Meredith had been living in this house for over two years, on her own, with no difficulties. Pete and I had spent chunks of time here, lasting from long weekends to an entire month, and never experienced any harassment.

Why now?

Chapter 19

Thursday, June 20

We spent the day Thursday adding finishing touches to the greenhouse: sealing joints on the plumbing, moving pots and other containers in, anchoring it into the ground, installing hooks and hanging tools from them. We made a trip to Home Depot for supplies; everyone we encountered there was friendly.

I had to remind myself not to relax my guard.

Tobias Rice called to let us know that Otto Pringle had pled guilty to property damage, which was a petty misdemeanor, and was sentenced to thirty days in jail. I said, "Will he be in long enough to dry out?"

Tobias said, "I hope so. Thing is, he claimed that he didn't remember who paid him to take out your cactus."

"Do you believe him?"

He sighed. "I'm not sure. But Otto's brain is pickled. It's entirely possible that he doesn't remember."

I thanked him and said goodbye.

Pete had chicken that he needed to cook, so he decided to make stir fry for dinner. He took out the cutting board; I said, "I'll get the mail."

"Okay." He started chopping.

I went out through the front door, reminding myself that raising the garage door used precious electricity, and jogged to the end of the driveway, where our oversized mailbox was mounted on a cement column reinforced with steel rods. If anyone tried a baseball bat on it, they'd break their arms.

I lowered the door with my left hand and started to reach with my right hand—and froze.

There was something lying on the two envelopes in the box.

I peered in, then recoiled. Someone had gifted us with a cake topper, two men in tuxedos holding hands.

Their bodies had been decapitated.

I stood staring at them for a moment, allowing my rage to build, then slammed the mailbox door closed and marched into the house. I snatched my phone from the kitchen table where I'd left it, located Tobias Rice's number, and called.

He answered, "Rice."

"Hi, Detective, it's Jamie Brodie. Sorry to bother you, but someone left a decapitated wedding cake topper in our mailbox."

Pete spun away from the counter, chopping knife in the air, staring at me. "What the *fuck?*"

Tobias said, "You haven't touched it, have you?"

"No, sir."

"I'll be there in ten minutes."

"Thank you." I clicked off.

Pete hadn't moved. "A cake topper?"

"Two men in tuxedos who are missing their heads. On top of the mail. I'm going to take a picture." I went back outside.

Pete followed, knife still in his hand. I guess he'd forgotten to lay it down. I opened the door and said, "Voila."

He slowly shook his head. "Son of a *bitch*."

"Whoever he is." I snapped photos and texted them to Kevin. *In our mailbox today*. He didn't answer immediately.

I started pacing the circle of the cul-de-sac, avoiding the patch of ground where Jacob Baldwin's body had lain. Pete lifted his hand and regarded the knife he held. "I should take this inside."

"Tobias would probably prefer that."

He went into the house. By the time he returned, Tobias was turning onto our street. He parked down the street, about a lot away, and walked to us. "Let's see this."

Pete opened the mailbox. I kept pacing but watched Tobias as he snapped photos of the figurine, then gloved up and removed it from the box. He examined it then dropped it into a sandwich-sized paper bag, which he immediately sealed. He carried the evidence to his car then returned to us. "This is getting old."

I snorted. "Imagine *my* thoughts on the subject."

"Yeah." He rubbed his temples. "We'll print it. Have you considered installing security cameras on the house?"

Pete said, "We're considering it now."

We hadn't discussed it, but I knew that we would as soon as we got inside. Tobias said, "Call Tularosa Security Systems. Al Berrocal is the owner, and a friend of mine. He'll be out here tomorrow."

I said, "We'll call him. Thank you."

Tobias went back to his car, just as my phone rang with the theme from *Hill Street Blues*. Kevin. I answered, "You got my text."

"What the holy *fuck?*"

"Tobias Reed just left. We're calling a security company he recommended to have cameras installed."

"It's not safe for you there."

I'd burned off some of my anger with my pacing, and I sighed. "What the hell am I supposed to do about it? Run?"

"Sell the fucking house to Steve and Meredith and *come home*."

"I don't think we're ready to consider that yet."

"What's it gonna take? Will one of you have to be injured or killed? Come *on*, Jamie."

Pete was watching me. I said, "We'll discuss it."

"You'd better."

"We will. Promise. I'm getting the hairy eyeball from Pete. I'll talk to you later."

"Let me know what Reed finds."

"I will." I said goodbye and hung up.

Pete asked, "We're not ready to consider *what* yet?"

"Selling the house to Steve and Meredith and going home."

Pete frowned, his eyes scanning the desert around us. "Let's go inside."

The dim, cool house felt like a sanctuary after the harsh heat and sunshine outside. Even though it was only 4:00, I grabbed a beer from the fridge and took a long drink. Pete said evenly, "What are your thoughts on that suggestion?"

“Right now, my thoughts are that we’d be surrendering to whoever these fuckers are. But I’m not sure that’s the best decision.”

Pete picked his knife up and began chopping with a vengeance. We’d have minced stir-fry if he kept it up. “Will you call the security guy?”

“Yup.” I located the number and dialed.

“Tularosa Security Systems, Al speaking.”

“Hi, Mr. Berrocal, my name is Jamie Brodie. Tobias Rice recommended that I call you. We’ve been having some vandalism at our house, and we need a security system installed.”

“What kind of vandalism?”

“Someone hammered crosses into our yard, someone chopped up some of our landscape plants… stuff like that.”

“Ah. Okay. I can come out tomorrow and give you an estimate, if that works for you.”

“Yes, sir, it sure does.”

“How about 9:00?”

“Perfect.” I gave him our address. “Thank you.”

“You bet. See you tomorrow.” He hung up.

I said to Pete, “9:00.”

He kept chopping. “Good.”

Chapter 20

Friday, June 21

Al Berrocal arrived right on time the next morning. After introductions, he surveyed our house and yard, making notes on a tablet computer. "How much money do you want to spend?"

I said, "As much as it takes."

He raised an eyebrow but didn't comment. "Do you want to be able to monitor the cameras online?"

"Yes, please."

"Okay. If you'll show me to a table and chair, I'll work up an estimate for you."

I led Al to the kitchen table. "Can I get you something to drink? We have bottled water from California."

"Can't pass that up."

On Al's recommendation, we chose a system with cameras covering every angle of the property, sensors on all the doors and windows, and cloud video storage. We could access and control it all from our phones. We scheduled installation for Monday.

I hoped that we wouldn't need it before then.

That afternoon we were on the back porch. Pete was napping. I was reading the *LA Times* online when Liz Nguyen texted.

Clinton's word of the day is skelf. An annoying or troublesome person.

Clinton Kenneally was our favorite patron, who came to the reference desk each afternoon to bestow a "word of the day" upon us. ***Ha! Who's he referring to?***

LOL any number of candidates. What are you doing?

Reading the LA newspaper. Pete's asleep. Have you talked to Kristen?

Yeah, she told me about your threats. Are you sure you want to live there?

We'll wear the fuckers down. Got an estimate for a security system this morning.

Ugh. Hate that you need it. She said that Jeff and Colin aren't going to see you next week.

Right.

Want us to come early?

Liz was married to Jon Eckhoff, Kevin's partner with the LAPD. I asked, ***Can you??***

Y. It's so slow at West LA right now, everyone's bored and cranky. We could be there Tuesday.

Sounds great to me. When Pete wakes up, I'll okay it with him.

Cool! I'm excited.

Me too.

Chapter 21

Saturday, June 22

On Saturday afternoon, Steve came over for a cookout. He grilled chicken and veggies, and Pete made twice-baked potatoes. After we ate, Meredith and I sent Pete and Steve to the back patio so that she and I could tackle the kitchen cleanup. She said, "Thanks again for letting me live in the house. It's been fantastic."

I snorted. "Until we got here."

She waved that off. "You've been here before, and nothing happened."

"True. But it was obviously out there, waiting for us."

"I'd like to say I'm surprised. But I'm not."

"Do you encounter prejudice here?"

She shrugged. "When I first arrived, yeah. Mostly sideways glances in the grocery store, you know. Now, I suppose people are used to seeing me."

"What did Steve say about that?"

"Steve is oblivious." Meredith shot me a sideways glance of her own. "Much like his brother."

"So it's a familial trait?"

"Christine seems to have bypassed it. But she's so tied up with Jack and the girls and the business that she's oblivious to Steve and Pete's obliviousness."

"Sounds about right. But I expect Steve to be oblivious. He's a physics geek. Pete's a psychologist. He's supposed to be more tuned in to his fellow man."

"Is he still in counseling?"

"No. But he might need to resume, after this experience."

She gave me a careful look. "I know you and he have been arguing about it."

"We have a basic difference of opinion. Pete thinks our issues will resolve spontaneously if we ignore them. I know they won't. And in the meantime, he's internalizing all these threats and insults. 'Cause that's what he does."

"You don't?"

"Nope. I get even."

"Good for you."

"Maybe." I glowered, scrubbing viciously at a pot. "It's trickier when you can't identify the culprits."

"But the cops will, eventually." Meredith smiled. "Be patient. I can tell you for sure that Tobias Rice is *pissed.* He'll find out who's behind your threats."

We both pondered that for a moment. I managed to restore the skillet to its pristine state and handed it to her. She accepted it solemnly. "Are you having second thoughts about moving here?"

I turned to face her. "I have not admitted this to anyone else."

"I won't say anything to anyone."

"Yes. I'm second-guessing this decision. We should have built this house near Albuquerque. Or maybe in San Diego County. I don't know." I wrung out the dishcloth and hung it over the faucet. "But I'm determined to live in this house, at least part time. Eventually."

"Steve would be disappointed if you didn't."

"I know, and I can't do that to Pete. But Kevin advised me to sell the house to you and Steve and come home. My family is *deeply* unhappy about all of this."

"I'm sure they are." Meredith dried the final dish and hung the towel next to the dishrag. "But I think we'll eventually learn who's behind this. Then all will be well."

"I hope you're right."

Chapter 23

Monday, June 24

When I woke up the next morning, the sky was already light, though the sun wasn't peeking over the mountains yet. Pete was still sleeping, his right arm across his eyes. I opened the French doors leading to the patio to let Ammo out ahead of me, pulled on shorts and a t-shirt, and followed him. At first, I didn't see where he'd gone, then I spotted him under one of the mesquite trees, sniffing at a small pile of...something.

I called, "Ammo?"

He glanced up at me but went back to sniffing whatever it was. I was a few yards away when he reached out with his mouth and took a tentative bite of whatever it was.

"Ammo, drop it! *DROP IT!*" I charged toward him.

He dropped something—but what was it? I grabbed his collar and dragged him away, then returned to the thing he'd nibbled at. "*Shit!*"

It was a mound of raw hamburger, about a pound's worth. Ammo had bit off a smidgen of the top of the mound; what he'd dropped seemed to be hamburger. The inside of the mound was full of pellets.

I didn't have my phone. I yelled, "Ammo, come!" I grabbed his collar and nearly dragged him back into the bedroom, where I yanked the covers off Pete and shook him. "*Wake up!* Ammo's been poisoned!"

"Huh? What?" Pete sat up, blinking. "*What?*"

"There's poisoned meat in the back yard, and he took a bite!" I grabbed my pillow and whacked Pete with it. "*GET UP! CALL THE VET!*"

Ammo was dancing around, excited by the sudden burst of activity. He looked okay so far, but… I grabbed my phone, then a zip top bag from the kitchen, and ran back to the mound of burger. I took photos from every conceivable angle, then turned the bag inside out and scooped up the entire mound of meat, including the bit that Ammo had had in his mouth.

Had he swallowed anything? I didn't know.

I ran back to the house, where Pete was on the phone while struggling to get his legs into a pair of shorts. "I don't know. My husband is the one… Here he is."

I snatched the phone. "Hello? This is Jamie Brodie. It was ground beef, about a pound of it, and the center is full of pellets. He took a bite, but I don't know if he swallowed any of the pellets."

A woman was on the other end of the phone. "Did you pick up the meat?"

"Yes. I'll bring it."

"Okay. I'll call the doctor right now, and we'll be waiting for you."

"Thank you." I clicked off. Pete was already on his feet and dressed, stuffing keys and his wallet into his pockets. He tossed my wallet at me. I caught it with one hand and ran for the garage. "Ammo, come!"

Ammo still thought we were playing some sort of delightful game. He cantered along beside me. I grabbed his leash from its hook beside the door that connected the laundry room to the garage. Pete was already in the garage; he threw the back door of the CR-V open. Ammo jumped in, and I leaped in right behind him.

Pete hit the garage door button and ran to the driver's side of the car. The door had barely cleared the roof of the car when he reversed out of the garage; the radio antenna twanged in protest as it hit the door. I threw the plastic bag with the hamburger into the front seat, then hooked Ammo's leash to his collar, fastened my own seatbelt, and held on.

The vet's office was right in the middle of town, only a few blocks from Meredith's law office. Pete drove as fast as he dared. As soon as he'd stopped the car by the front door, I jumped out. Ammo followed. He still was acting okay, as far as I could tell.

Pete was right on our heels, carrying the plastic bag. The vet tech we'd met before, wearing scrubs with cartoon kittens on them—why was I noticing that *now?*—held the door to a room open. "Right in here."

Dr. Smith reached for the plastic bag. "Lift him onto the exam table, please?"

I scooped Ammo up and deposited him onto the steel table. "Ammo, down."

He obediently lay down. Dr. Smith asked, "How much do you think he ate?"

"I'm not sure if he swallowed any of it. I yelled at him to drop it, and he spit that bit out." I pointed. "I looked down into the top of the ball of hamburger and saw the pellets."

Dr. Smith squished around on the bag until he could see the pellets. "I was afraid of that. We'll have to make him throw up."

Pete asked, "What is it?"

"Rat poison. Have him sit up, if you would?"

Pete gasped. I felt like I'd been stabbed in the heart. I said, "Ammo, sit. Good boy."

Ammo sat. Dr. Smith produced a bottle and poured out a dose into a plastic cup. "Hold his head up, please."

I raised Ammo's nose into the air. "Good boy, Ammo, good boy. Drink this nasty stuff like a good boy."

"Supposedly, it doesn't taste that bad." Dr. Smith expertly pried Ammo's mouth open and poured the liquid in. I let go of his head. Ammo spluttered but seemed to swallow it all.

Pete had dropped into a chair in the corner. His head was in his hands. I stroked Ammo's head and ears, murmuring, "Good boy," doing my best not to think beyond the next few minutes.

Dr. Smith said, "It'll take about ten minutes to work. Had he eaten breakfast yet?"

"No."

"Good." Dr. Smith looked back and forth between Pete and me. "Don't worry. He couldn't possibly have absorbed much of it. Even if he did manage to swallow some, we can treat it with

Vitamin K." He picked up the plastic bag. "In the meantime, I'll sample this."

I said, "We want the police involved."

Dr. Smith nodded. "Sure. I'll call them." He left the room.

Pete came to the exam table and buried his face in Ammo's neck. "I'm sorry, buddy. I'm so sorry."

I dug my phone from my pocket and texted Jeff, including the photo I'd taken of the pellets. ***Ammo might have been poisoned. Got into a chunk of hamburger that had been thrown over the wall. Vet says it's rat poison.***

He responded immediately. ***OMFG. It sure is. Inducing vomiting?***

Yeah. I don't think he got much, if any.

It's treatable, even if he did. Vitamin K daily for 30 days.

If he has to be treated, I'm coming to Oceanside and bringing him with me.

OK. Did you call the cops?

Vet is calling.

Think this is those church people? Kev filled me in last night.

Don't know. So far hasn't been their style.

Let me know.

I sent back a thumbs up and said to Pete, "Jeff says treatment lasts thirty days. If he has to be treated, I'm taking him to Oceanside."

Pete nodded numbly. "I'm so sorry…"

There was a knock on the door, and Officer Smallwood stuck his head through. "Doc Smith says your dog might be poisoned?"

I said, "We're waiting for him to puke."

Smallwood closed the door behind him. "Is the doc through here?"

"Yeah. I took pictures of the hamburger in place, if you want them."

"Yes, I'll need those. Hang on." He went in search of Dr. Smith.

Ammo was panting and appeared to be somewhat less happy than he'd been when we arrived. Maybe he was starting to feel sick. Pete was still stroking him, crooning soothingly to him.

Tears were running down Pete's face. I said, "Honey, it's not your fault."

He shook his head, bit his lip, and kept talking to Ammo.

It wasn't our fault. But it sure as shit was *someone's* fault. If the cops couldn't find out through official channels, I'd have a discussion with Tobias Reed.

Ammo stood up and started the racking, hacking sound that preceded hurling. I positioned myself behind his head, opposite from Pete. Dr. Smith came back to the room; Officer Smallwood followed, but stayed in the doorway.

Dr. Smith, brave man, stood in front of Ammo with a bucket. Ammo heaved a few more times then proceeded to puke. And puke. And puke. I wouldn't have been surprised to see his toenails land in the bucket. He finally ran out of gastric juice and dry heaved for a while, then collapsed onto the tabletop, spent.

Pete was stroking and murmuring, "Poor baby. Good boy. You're such a good puppy." Dr. Smith, Officer Smallwood, and I peered into the bucket.

Dr. Smith said, "I'll strain this to be sure, but I don't see anything solid at all. I think he must have spit everything out."

I sagged in relief. Smallwood said, "Great news. Do you want to email me those pictures you took?"

"Yes." I typed in his email address as he recited it, then attached the photos and hit Send. "Any idea who might have done this? It seems beyond what church people would get up to."

"I agree." Smallwood's expression didn't reveal much. "I have some ideas. We'll process the evidence, see if it shows us anything. I'll come out to your house in a bit, see if there are useful footprints or other evidence."

"Thank you."

"No problem." He left through the door to the waiting room.

Dr. Smith had taken the bucket to the back; now he returned. "Nothing solid in there at all. I'd say we're safe."

"If he'd swallowed any part of a pellet, it wouldn't have been digested that fast, would it?"

"Not entirely, no. There would be at least a fragment left. I don't think he even swallowed any of the hamburger." Dr. Smith ruffled Ammo's ears. "Poor fella. Keep him quiet today. Let him drink as much as he wants this morning, then around noon try feeding him some plain mashed potatoes. See how he does with that. I'll call you this afternoon."

"Thank you."

"You're welcome." He tousled Ammo's ears one more time then returned to the back.

Pete didn't seem capable of coordinated thought or movement. I lifted Ammo from the table and gently deposited him on the floor, then opened the door to the waiting room. "Ready to go home, buddy?"

At the word *home*, he perked up and began tugging on the leash. I handed the leash to Pete. "Want to put him in the car? I'll pay."

Pete didn't speak but took the leash and went outside. I stopped at the reception desk, where the woman in the cute kitten scrubs gave me a worried smile. "Everything's okay, then?"

"Seems to be." I lowered my voice, even though we were alone. "Who around here poisons animals?"

"There aren't many. Josh will find 'em, whoever did it."

"Josh?"

"Smallwood. He and his wife do animal rescue. He *hates* animal cruelty." She lowered her voice as well. "If he finds out who did it, he'll fix it up. Don't you worry."

I held up my hand. "The less I know, the better."

"You bet. Doc Smith will call you later today."

I signed the credit card slip and went outside. Pete had started the car and had the a/c running but was in the passenger seat. Ammo was resting his head on the console between the seats. I climbed into the driver's seat. "Are you okay?"

"No."

I squeezed his forearm then buckled my seatbelt and backed out of the parking space. “Ammo’s okay. That’s what matters.”

“He had dry heaves again in the parking lot.”

“Poor puppy.” We were at a stoplight; I handed my phone to Pete. “Text Jeff and tell him what’s up.”

By the time we got home it was 8:45. Al Berrocal would arrive in fifteen minutes to install our security system. Ammo lapped from his water bowl for a minute then lay down on the cool tile of the kitchen floor and went to sleep. Pete dropped onto a barstool and rested his head on his arms. “Fuuuuuuck.”

Now that the fear for Ammo was subsiding, what remained in my brain was cold fury. “You got that right. As soon as Al is done with the installation, I’m outta here.”

Pete’s head snapped up. “What?”

“*MOTHERFUCKERS TRIED TO KILL OUR DOG!*”

He blinked. I threw my hands in the air. “*I AM DONE*. Assholes want me gone, I’m gettin’ the fuck outta Dodge. I’m gonna take Ammo to Jeff, then I’ll come back and start packing.”

Pete was staring at me as if he’d never seen me. It was true, he never had seen me in this state. He said, “The vet said to keep Ammo quiet today. And to feed him mashed potatoes at noon. You can’t go today.”

Damn. I shook my finger at him. “No fair using logic against me. Then we’ll go tomorrow.”

“Jon and Liz are coming tomorrow.”

“They can turn around and go back.”

“Jamie.”

“What?”

“Please don’t leave me.”

“*What?* I’m not leaving *you*. You’re coming, too.”

He closed his eyes. Tears began leaking out from under his lashes.

Well, shit. I hated it when he cried. “Honey?”

He scrubbed at his face. “Maybe this is twisted logic. I don’t know. But I feel like if I leave, that I’m giving up my last chance for a close relationship with Steve. You'll be running back to your family. I'll be running away from mine."

I sighed deeply, sudden exhaustion washing over me. That's the primary reason that we were here, after all—for Pete and Steve. He kept talking. "You're my rock here, Jamie. If you give up, then I don't know what… how… I don't know *anything*."

I went to him and folded him in my arms. We stood there, holding each other, until the doorbell rang.

Once Al and his crew were underway outside, I realized that I was hungry. I pulled bacon and eggs from the fridge and got out a couple of frying pans. "Pete? Do you want breakfast?"

"Not really."

"Bacon makes everything better."

He didn't respond to that. Maybe he'd want some once he smelled it. I arranged strips of bacon in one pan and melted butter in the other. I was beating eggs together with half and half when Pete asked, "You couldn't have stopped Ammo from eating it?"

"No. I hollered at him to stop, but he bit off the top anyway. He seemed to know there was something wrong with it, but he couldn't overcome his attraction to raw meat. He's a Lab. We're lucky he didn't just gulp down the whole thing. Which is probably what the poisoner was counting on."

"You shouldn't have let him go out ahead of you."

I stopped, dripping fork in the air. "Are you trying to blame *me* for this? Because it sure sounds like that's what you're working up to."

"No, of course I'm not blaming you. I'm just saying that you—*we*—shouldn't let Ammo out without us."

"Well, *obviously*, I'm not gonna do it again. But we've both done it dozens of times before. Who could have guessed that they, whoever they are, would go after Ammo?"

"*We* should have guessed."

"But *we* didn't. *You're* the one who's been downplaying everything that's happened."

Pete reddened. "I have *not...*" His phone rang, and he answered. "Hey. What's up? *What?*" His face reddened even more. "Who was it? Did you call Tobias Rice? No, we had to make an emergency run to the vet. There was rat poison wrapped in hamburger in our back yard this morning."

Pete held the phone away from his ear; I could hear Steve swearing. When he stopped, Pete spoke again. "He seems fine. Apparently, he didn't eat any. Yes, Josh Smallwood came and took everything into evidence. I don't know. No, Jamie was with him. He says not."

Wonderful. Steve was blaming me too. I gritted my teeth. Pete said, "All right. Let me know. Bye."

I said, "What happened?"

"Someone ran over Steve's mailbox and destroyed it."

"What the *hell?* Does he know who?"

"The paint matches one of his neighbors' cars."

"Steve thinks that it was my fault that Ammo ate the hamburger. Same as you."

"He didn't say that."

"He didn't have to."

Pete sighed deeply. He looked as if he'd aged five years in the past three hours. "I don't blame you, Jamie. I'm blaming myself."

"Why? It's not your fault either, any more than it is mine. Whoever tossed that meat over the wall is who's to blame."

"I know. I just... I can't believe *any* of this."

I turned back to the stove. "Steve called Tobias?"

"Yeah."

"What kind of idiot *is* that neighbor? Did he think Steve would accept a lame excuse? Would leave the cops out of it? And Tobias lives on the same street, right?"

"Right. Obviously, the neighbor doesn't know Steve very well. And his car is a bright yellow Kia. No one else on the street has that color."

"Will Steve press charges?"

"Probably." Pete shot a sideways glance at me. "You know, you're reacting to these incidents like a cop would."

"What? Nah."

"Yes, you are. Your first instinct with each of these incidents has been to take photos. You repeated details to Dr. Smith and Josh Smallwood like a cop would. Your immediate thought is whether or not to press charges."

"You've trained me well."

"Not me. Kevin."

I considered that. "No, you too. You still react to most stuff like a cop. Hell, everyone around me does. *Liz* thinks like a cop now."

That produced a slight grin. "Seriously?"

"Oh my *God*. I think she and Jon discuss cases over dinner. She wants to write a paper with him about democracy and policing."

"Pfft. They could write a *book* about that." Pete traced the pattern of the wood grain on the top of the table. "There's someone out there who wants to hurt us."

I intended to let Pete think through this himself. "Yes."

"Someone more than that church congregation, assuming that's who pulled the prior stunts. What they did was penny-ante compared to this."

"Yeah."

He raised his head to look at me, his expression sorrowful. "What're we gonna do?"

"If we're going to stay, we have to let the cops do their jobs."

"You said…"

"I know. We're going to stay. For now." Now that my rage had subsided and I could think straight, I was even more determined to see this through.

"We need to get you a handgun."

"See, now *you're* thinking like a cop. Do you believe another gun is the answer?"

"I don't know *what* the answer is."

"Neither do I." I loaded a plate with bacon and eggs and sat across from him. "Liz and Jon are coming tomorrow. We have another week's worth of work left on the house and garden. Let's get through this next week. Once we're at home, when we're safe and sane, we'll decide what to do long-term."

"Home." He dropped my gaze and traced another wood grain pattern. "Home will always be California to you. You'll never think of this place as home."

"Pete. This is our *dream* house. I *want* to live in this house."

"But?"

I sighed. "But right now? I wish we'd built in San Diego County. Or at least in northern New Mexico."

"We can't move this house, like your dad moved his."

"I know." The doorbell rang; I squeezed his left hand. "Let's not discuss it now. I need to wash dishes, and Al probably needs to come inside to work."

"I'll wash." Pete squeezed my hand in response and slid out from behind the table. "You talk to Al."

"Deal."

By the time Al and his guys were at work indoors, Officer Smallwood had arrived. He found a few shoe prints on the outer side of the wall, about where someone would have stood to throw the hamburger over. He took photos and measurements, then left. I got a shovel from the garage then went to the back yard and dug a wide perimeter hole where the raw hamburger had lain, tossing each shovelful of soil into a bucket lined with a plastic bag for disposal.

I would *not* take any chances.

Al and his crew completed the installation by noon. He gave us a brief tutorial on using the system then left.

We ate lunch on the front porch, shotgun propped between us, watching the neighborhood. Ammo seemed fine; he ate a bowl full of mashed potatoes for lunch then passed out on the cool tile in the kitchen.

Neither of us said much. I vacillated between imagining revenge fantasies against Ammo's poisoner and considering options to living here full time.

None of them were workable. Pete was determined to garden, making exhaustive use of the raised beds, greenhouse, beehives, and chicken coop. Nothing other than full time occupancy would allow for that. Not to mention… Steve was his family.

I remembered what I'd said to him last December. *Wherever you go, I will go also*. I'd meant it.

I still did.

I'd switched from thinking to cloud-watching when a car pulled onto the street. When it was halfway to the house, I reached over and lifted the shotgun, laying it across my lap.

The car turned in the circle and parked in front of our house. Pete said, "No one ever parks in the driveway."

"Suits me."

A guy climbed from the driver's seat. Unless someone was lying down in his back seat, he was alone. He was probably around Pete's age, early forties, with thick brown hair, wearing chinos and a polo shirt. He stopped halfway down the driveway and waved. "Hello, Mr. Brodie? Mr. Ferguson?"

I rested my hand on the stock of the shotgun. Pete said, "Yeah?"

"I'm Devin Maldonado, from the Alamogordo Daily News. I was a friend of Joey Norman's."

"Hold on." I picked up my phone to search and confirmed that there was a reporter for the Daily News by that name.

He didn't move any closer. "I don't blame you for being cautious."

Pete asked, "What can we do for you?"

"I'd like to talk to you about this harassment you've been experiencing."

I said, "With the intent of writing an article?"

"Yes, but also with the intent of shining a bright light on this behavior. The public might be more likely to cooperate with the police if they see you as real people, not just whatever exists in their minds when they think 'gay.'"

Pete and I looked at each other. I shrugged. He said, "Okay, let's talk."

Devin approached cautiously, eyeing the shotgun. "I'll show you ID, if you like."

I said, "Sure."

He tugged a driver's license from his wallet and handed it over. I glanced at it, noting that the address was in the northern section of town, then handed it back. "Were you and Danny close?"

"We didn't socialize much. Occasionally we'd go for a drink and talk about stories. But I liked him a lot." He blinked. "I miss him. Most of us at the newspaper do."

I noted the word *most*. Pete said, "Danny didn't only write for the Daily News. Do you?"

"Yes. I'm one of the few."

I said, "So. What do you want to know?"

He tapped on his phone. "According to the police log, you've had four incidents so far. A threatening note in your newspaper, crosses in your yard, destruction of property, and a headless cake topper in your mailbox."

Pete said, "And this morning, someone tried to poison our dog."

Devin sucked in a breath. "*Shit.* What happened?"

I said, "Rat poison in hamburger, tossed over the wall into the back yard."

"Is he okay?"

"Yes. He didn't eat any of the pellets, thank God."

Pete said, "It's one thing to harass adult humans. But to attack a defenseless animal? Who happens to be a retired Marine?"

Devin's eyes widened. "He's a retired Marine?"

I said, "He was a bomb-sniffing dog. We retrained him as a cadaver dog."

Pete added, "He's a special fella."

"He found Danny Norman, right?"

I said, "That's right. We'd like to offer his services to Alamogordo Search and Rescue once we live here full time. Unless someone poisons him first."

Pete shot me a sideways glance. I ignored him.

Devin asked, "How does all of this make you feel?"

I snorted. "It makes me feel sorry that we decided to live in this town. Not sure you should print that, though."

Pete said, "It makes me sad to think that there are people here who are so afraid of the unknown that they're willing to commit criminal acts. And it's sad that there are people who can't think of anything better to do with their time. There's so much need in the world—in this town—and some folks choose to spread fear and hate instead of helping. I don't understand that mindset."

I understood that mindset perfectly well, but I knew what Pete was going for, so I kept my mouth shut. Devin plowed on. "Tell me about your backgrounds."

I said, "We both grew up in blue collar homes. My dad's a Marine gunnery sergeant." I purposely didn't say *was*. Maybe people would be more kindly disposed to the family of an active duty serviceman. "Pete's dad was a machinist at Edwards Air Force Base. My mom died when I was a baby; Pete's parents divorced when he was young. We're products of the public school system. We were both only able to attend college thanks to scholarships."

Devin nodded as he typed into his phone. "Good stuff. Athletic scholarships?"

"Yes. Baseball for Pete, rugby for me." I figured I wouldn't mention my academic scholarships. Too elitist.

"And you both work in public education, right?"

"Right. I'm at UCLA and Pete teaches online for Arizona State."

"Why did you decide to build a house in Alamogordo?""

Pete said, "My brother lives here. Steve Ferguson. He works at Holloman."

"Who built your house?"

"Mitch Campbell of Desert Green Construction in Las Cruces."

"Why do you have that big adobe wall?"

"To keep wildlife out of the vegetable garden. We're not doing anything immoral back there."

“So you’re not considering leaving.”

I’d never admit it to the public. “No, we are not. Pete’s an ex-cop. I was raised by Marines. We don’t run.”

Devin’s ears perked up. “You were a cop?”

Pete said, “Yes. A patrol officer in Los Angeles.”

“Has the Alamogordo Police Department been helpful?”

“Yes. Extremely. We’ve had immediate responses to our calls and have been treated with respect and concern.”

“But no one’s been apprehended yet.”

Pete said, “Not yet. The police will find the criminals eventually. I know they’d appreciate help from the public, though.”

Devin said, “Absolutely. I’ll emphasize that in the article. I must ask… How were you able to build this house?”

I gave him an abbreviated version of the Gavin and Randall Barkley saga. He nodded solemnly as he took notes. “Okay, thank you. May I meet your dog?”

He met Ammo, took pictures of him and of us—with Ammo strategically placed between us—looking straight into the camera. Pete’s expression was determined, yet hopeful.

I just looked pissed off.

Devin thanked us for our time. “The article will be in tomorrow’s edition.”

I said, “We’ll look forward to it.”

Steve and Meredith arrived at dinnertime, bearing pizza. As we ate around the kitchen table Pete asked Steve, “What happened with your mailbox?”

He snorted. “The neighbor—his name’s Leland Hart—was charged with reckless driving. He offered to pay for the mailbox. I told him to keep his money and filed an insurance claim.”

Meredith said, “Why not take his money?”

“Because paying for it would allow him to clear his conscience. I don’t want him to have a clear conscience.”

I asked, “What do you know about this guy?”

“He goes to church. I don’t know where. He and his next-door neighbor are always arguing about a fence. He works at the wastewater treatment plant, and his wife is a home health aide. They have adult children who went away to college and never came back."

"Could you find out where he goes to church? If he goes to that Holiness church, maybe that'll give the cops a reason to start pulling those people in for questioning."

Steve shrugged. "I could ask around, I guess."

Pete said, "We were visited by a newspaper reporter today." He told about our interview with Devin Maldonado.

Meredith said, "I know who he is. I've seen him around the courthouse."

I picked up another slice of pizza. "He said he wanted to encourage the public to come forward. I hope it works that way."

The others all murmured agreement.

Chapter 24

Tuesday, June 25

The next morning, I hustled outside to retrieve the newspaper first thing, anxious to see what Devin Maldonado had written. Meredith, Pete, and I read it together over bowls of oatmeal.

Devin had done a fine job. He played up our military connections, Pete's law enforcement past, and the horror of Ammo's attempted poisoning, and played down the house and inheritance. He presented us as a couple of average middle-class guys. He'd also obtained a quote from the chief of police, Cliff Warner, who urged the public to come forward with information leading to arrests and stated that Joey Norman had guaranteed $10,000 for such information. He then said, "Mr. Brodie and Mr. Ferguson are exactly the sort of folks that we should be welcoming in this town. Folks who bring resources to our community instead of draining them. Whoever these perpetrators are should be deeply ashamed at their behavior."

Meredith said, "Chief Warner took a subtle shot at undocumented immigrants there."

I said, "True. Maybe he was just trying to make us sound more palatable."

"Maybe. What time are Liz and Jon getting here?"

"Probably around dinnertime."

Pete said, "I'll make something in the slow cooker. Then dinner will be ready whenever we are."

"Sounds good." Meredith shoved back from the table. "I'm off to the gym. See you guys later."

Pete carried his bowl to the sink and began to rummage in the fridge for dinner ingredients. I scanned the rest of the paper. There was a short article about the Jacob Baldwin case, also written by Devin, which basically stated what we already knew—that at this point the cops were stymied.

Then something else caught my eye.

“Hey, Pete, listen to this. There’s a firearms safety class being offered at the gun range Thursday afternoon.”

He snorted. “You don’t need a firearms safety class.”

“*I’m* aware of that. No one else in town is.”

My dad’s final rank in the Marines had been Master Gunnery Sergeant, and he’d taught weapons and tactics to recruits and SEALS at Camp Pendleton for nearly his entire career, after his two tours in Vietnam. He’d also started taking his sons to the range as soon as we were big enough to hold a gun steady. I’d gotten out of practice during my college and grad school years, but once I’d returned to the States from England, I’d resumed shooting. I still went to the range at least twice a month with Kevin or Pete.

Kevin still held the record at the LAPD Academy for shooting accuracy. I was nearly as skilled as he was.

Pete shook his head. “What do you intend to prove?”

“I don’t want to prove anything. I want to reinforce Devin’s message, that we’re not a pair of pearl-clutching femmes. Not that there’s *anything* wrong with that.”

He chuckled. I said, “They want us to be afraid. That’s what all of this has been about, right? I wanna turn the tables. I want *them* to be afraid.”

He turned to face me, leaning against the counter, his arms crossed. “My brain must be totally fucked up. Because I suspect that this is a lousy idea, but I can’t think of a reason why.”

“Hey. With my luck, I’ll probably be the only guy that signs up for the class.”

He snorted and went back to his preparations. I called the gun range and spoke to a woman who didn’t seem to recognize my name when I registered for the class.

Good.

Pete decided on chicken and dumplings for dinner. The day was hotter than usual, so we spent it mostly inside. Pete read about beekeeping and criminal justice; I painted the baseboards in the middle guest room.

Liz and Jon arrived at about a quarter of five. They were current regarding our travails, thanks to Kevin and Kristen, so we didn't have to update them. Meredith got home about twenty minutes later, and we sat down to eat. During dinner, talk turned to the Jacob Baldwin case.

Liz said, "He's the brother-in-law of a cop. Looks like that would turn up the investigative heat."

I said, "I know Brian is doing the best he can. But if they can't find where he came from... what can they do?"

Jon swiped half a dumpling through gravy and admired it for a moment. "Not much. Their best shot will be to find that airplane."

Meredith said, "If they're flying at night, it must be someone who's familiar with our mountains."

Jon nodded, his mouth full of dumpling. Liz said, "What about trying to identify that chemical in the victim's blood? Could they figure out where that came from?"

Meredith asked, "Is that possible? If they can't identify it?"

Pete said, "Probably not."

After dinner, we gathered on the front porch to watch the sun set, the shotgun leaning against the wall. Jon, Pete, and Meredith were discussing what Meredith knew about the drug trade in Otero County. I said to Liz, "Do you have Google Earth on your computer?"

Liz owned a massive laptop with a 17.3-inch screen, which she'd brought with her. She said, "Of course. Why?"

"I just want to check something."

She went inside and returned with the computer. She booted it up then tapped on the Google Earth icon. "What are we looking for?"

"An airstrip. Search for Piñon, New Mexico."

"Haven't the cops done this?"

"Sure. Two extra sets of eyes never hurt, right?"

We spent the next hour sitting next to each other on the top step of the porch, scouring the southeastern quadrant of New Mexico for anything that looked like an airstrip, but saw nothing.

Finally, Liz closed her laptop with a sigh. "Maybe he lands on a road."

"Nah, the kid that Brian talked to, who'd been at the camp, said they took him to an airstrip on the other side of the mountain from the camp." I waved my hand at the screen. "Maybe we're searching in the wrong place."

"Your young guy walked from where?"

I showed Liz the location of Route 506, where the bloodhounds had lost Jacob's scent. "But the camp isn't necessarily on 506. Who knows how far he walked before he came to the road?"

"He couldn't have jumped into a moving pickup truck. The truck must have been stopped somewhere."

"Yeah." I rubbed my eyes. "But it wasn't necessarily even on 506. It could have been on one of these little side roads. It could have been *anywhere*."

Liz gave me a sideways look. "You're taking this personally."

"Damn straight. *I* found Jacob in the street." I pointed back over my shoulder toward the mountains to the east. "Somewhere out there, kids are being abused in the same manner that Jacob was, and the cops can't find them. It *pisses me off*."

Jon had gone inside a moment ago; now he returned, carrying two bottles of beer. He handed one to Pete and dropped into his chair. "Infrared."

Liz and I responded in unison. "Huh?"

"The police have surely been searching at night with infrared cameras. They may have even deployed drones."

Liz grunted. "Then they must be looking in the wrong place."

I said, "After all this time? Surely they've covered the entire area of possibility by now."

Jon nodded. "There are ways to block it. Staying entirely indoors, for example."

Liz said, "They have to come out *sometime*. When new kids arrive. To get supplies. To chop wood."

"Right. But if the drones aren't looking then…"

I sighed. “What you’re saying is that the cops are doing everything that can be done.”

Jon tipped his beer bottle at me. “Yes. At this point, they’ll just have to get lucky.”

Chapter 25

Wednesday, June 26

The next morning Meredith was gone before anyone else was awake; she was spending the next couple of days at her firm's headquarters in Albuquerque. Liz cooked breakfast, a marvelous Hawaiian take on huevos rancheros. Over breakfast, I mentioned the gun safety course scheduled for tomorrow afternoon.

Liz waved her fork in the air. "Ooh! I wanna go."

Jon said, "You don't need a firearms safety course."

Pete said, "Exactly what I said."

Liz made a "pfft" sound. "I know, but I want to keep Jamie company. Somebody needs to, right?"

Pete snorted. "Yeah. Somebody needs to."

Once Liz had registered for the firearms course, we piled into our CR-V for a jaunt to the pistachio farm. We toured the ranch, then went into the gift shop. I knew that Liz was a pistachio fan, and I had taken bags of them back to LA for her on previous visits. She marveled at all of the different flavors and bought about a dozen bags.

It was close to noon when we left the building. I was behind Pete, talking to Liz about where we might eat lunch, and bumped into him when he stopped short.

All four tires on the car were slashed.

We all sucked in a breath...then I exploded. "God *damn* it! *Fuck* these people!" I checked the windshield for a note. Nothing.

Liz gasped. "Those *fucking assholes!*"

Jon said, "Well, now." There was something dangerous in his tone that I'd never heard before.

Pete was silent, staring at the car.

Liz turned in a circle. "This parking lot is half full. It's broad daylight. And no one saw anything?" She shouted in the direction of the shop. "*No one fucking saw anything?*"

I pulled my phone from my pocket and called Tobias Rice. He answered, "Dr. Brodie. What's happened now?"

I told him.

"I'll be right there."

Jon circled the car from a couple of yards away, squatting occasionally to look at something on the ground. Liz paced, muttering imprecations against the entire state of New Mexico under her breath.

Pete still hadn't moved or spoken. I shoved my phone back in my pocket. "Pete?"

He just shook his head.

Tobias—and to my surprise, Brian—arrived in about ten minutes. Tobias immediately began snapping photos. I asked Brian, "What are you doing here?"

"This is outside the city limits. Technically we should have called the sheriff."

"Yet here you are."

"Yet here I am. Let me talk to your friend." Meaning Jon.

Jon, Brian, and Tobias conferred for several minutes. Tobias dusted the fenders for prints and didn't find any but bagged a fresh-looking cigarette butt that Jon had found nearby. He deposited the evidence in his car then walked back toward us. "I'll speak with the people inside."

He headed for the gift shop. I said to Brian and Jon, "We won't find them, will we?"

Jon said, "It depends. If they, whoever they are, just got lucky and spotted your car parked here, then probably not. But if they followed you here? We might."

That got Pete's attention. "We're not being *followed.*"

"Then how did they know where you were?"

Pete turned and walked toward the pistachio grove.

We all watched him go. Liz said, "Not good."

No kidding. I asked Brian, "Can I call Triple A now?"

"Sure."

The towing company estimated that they'd arrive in a half hour. Tobias found no one who'd seen anything; he left. Brian stayed. He and Jon went to stand in the shade of the building and were soon deep in conversation. Liz was still pacing but had stopped swearing. I took pictures of the tires, then went to find Pete.

He'd wandered to the back of the gift shop building and was standing at the edge of the pistachio grove, looking west. In the distance, the dunes of White Sands were shimmering, a white streak at the base of the mountains.

I stood beside him. "Gorgeous view."

"Yeah."

"What are you thinking?"

"What is there to think? We're helpless against this."

I was glad that he was acknowledging the gravity of our situation but dismayed at his emotional reaction. "We are *not* helpless, sweetheart. We are gonna find these assholes and punish them severely."

He didn't respond. I said softly, "Pete."

"When is the tow truck coming?"

"Soon."

"Come get me when it's here." Dismissing me.

I looked at him for a moment, then said, "Okay." What else could I say?

I went back to the front of the building, where Liz intercepted me. "Is Pete okay?"

"Nope."

She bit her lip. "What are you gonna do?"

"Keep encouraging him to talk, I guess. I don't know what else to do."

"Maybe I can get through to him."

"That's not a bad idea."

She slugged me lightly in the shoulder. "Ideas. I haz them."

I huffed a laugh. "What would I do without you?"

"Let's never find out."

I gently slugged her shoulder. "Deal."

The tow truck arrived on schedule. The driver was a man of few words. He winched the car onto the flatbed and said, "Where'm I taking this?"

Brian said, "I'd suggest Discount Tire."

I said, "Discount Tire it is."

"Okay. One of you ridin' with me?"

Jon said, "I will."

The rest of us piled into Brian's cruiser and followed the tow truck into town. At the tire dealer, I conferred with the manager about the type of tires we wanted. He asked, "You gonna file insurance?"

"Um…" I glanced at Pete, who shook his head slightly. "No."

"Okay. We'll have it for ya in a couple of hours."

"Thanks."

Brian dropped us off at the house. Jon disappeared into his and Liz's bedroom. I went straight to the cabinet where we kept the liquor, uncapped a bottle of Glenmorangie and poured two glasses. I handed one to Pete, then offered the other to Liz.

"Ew. Do you have wine?"

"Yes, ma'am. We are a full-service establishment."

Pete was studying his glass. "It's not even two yet."

"It's almost five in Nova Scotia."

He snorted but slugged back a mouthful of the whiskey.

Jon returned, wearing his holster and gun. Liz frowned at him as she poured a healthy serving of white wine. "Really?"

"This is an open carry state." He accepted my offer of the glass of whiskey. "I'll be open carrying on the front porch."

Liz said, "I'll come with you."

I took a bottle of beer from the fridge for myself. Pete was still gazing into the depths of his glass. I said, "Hey, hon."

He looked up at me. "What?"

"Do you want to drink here, or outside?"

"Um. Outside, I guess." He reached around me for the bottle of Glenmorangie and carried it with him to the front door.

"I'll be there in a sec." I opened the door to the back patio. Ammo had been dancing around our legs; I took him out to do his business, sticking to his side to make sure his path was clear, then gave him a treat and joined the others on the porch.

Pete and Liz were in one set of chairs; both were already halfway through their drinks. I hoped that maybe Liz could draw Pete into conversation, and sat down beside Jon.

He was deceptively relaxed, his feet propped on the porch rail, his eyes hidden behind mirrored shades. I said, "You look like a modern-day gunslinger."

He affected a Western drawl. "I reckon that's what I am, pardner."

"What are you thinking?"

He glanced at me sideways; I could see his eyes behind the edge of his sunglasses. "Wrong question. The question is, what are *you* thinking?"

"I'm thinking this fucking harassment needs to *stop. Now.*"

"Mm hm."

"Except I don't know how to make that happen. What were you and Brian talking about?"

"He's gonna make an informal call to the FBI. They have a mandate to investigate hate crimes."

"Nothing that's happened is serious enough to involve the Feds, though, is it?"

"Technically, no. Everything so far, except for Ammo's attempted poisoning, is a misdemeanor."

"Is the poisoning a felony?"

"Yup. Extreme animal cruelty, under which poisoning falls, is a fourth-degree felony in New Mexico."

"You looked it up?"

"I was curious." Another sideways glance, this one with a slight smirk. "Anyway, Brian's gonna invite the local Feds to visit this unfair city and have an informal chat about...stuff."

"Do you think there's one person, or group, behind all of this?"

"Yes. It feels to me like a coordinated effort. Mostly because of the spacing of the incidents."

I took a long drink of beer. "I'd like to march into that Holiness church on Sunday, right in the middle of the service, and tell 'em all that they're going straight to hell."

"I have no trouble picturing that. Problem is, are you sure it's them?"

"No." I sighed. "As Kristen pointed out when they were here, there are thirty-three fundamental, evangelical, etcetera churches in this town. It could be any of 'em. Or none of 'em. That's the problem. We don't enough fucking *evidence*."

"Actually, you do. The problem is that there's no one to tie it to yet."

I studied the depths of my beer bottle. "Will there ever be?"

Jon sipped at his whiskey and smacked his lips. "Allow me to present to you with what is, I believe, the central question to be answered. The *essential* question. *Why now?*"

"That thought has occurred to me."

He saluted me with his glass. "Great minds. Let's dig there for a minute. You've spent extended periods of time here before, right?"

"Right. From long weekends when the house was being built, to an entire month at the end of my sabbatical in 2017. We were here for two weeks last December. *Nothing happened*."

"Meh. Let's discount December. It's cold, people are busy. You were here for an entire month, same approximate time of year, two years ago."

"And that's significant how?"

"I'd be curious to see which of those thirty-three churches of Kristen's did not exist two years ago."

I stared at him, mouth open. "That's brilliant."

He grinned. "Aw, shucks."

"How do we find that out, though?"

"Pfft. You're the research librarian; how would you find that out?"

I smacked myself in the forehead. "Duh. Websites."

"Yup. You and Lizzie get to work on that later. You'll have the answer in no time."

"Okay. But what if they've all been established for years?"

"Well, we haven't fully answered our question. What's different about *now?*"

I gazed across the street, intending to think about it, and realized the answer was right in front of me. "Jacob Baldwin."

"Yes."

"But all I did was find his body. If he'd made it to the end of the street, someone else would've found him."

Jon drained his glass and set it aside. "Let's pretend for a minute. I am the owner and operator of a highly profitable gay conversion camp. I'm feeling good about my life choices. My camp is hidden away in the mountains where no one will ever find it, or so I believe. No one outside the camp itself even knows that it's in New Mexico. I can see early retirement in my future. Maybe on Bali. But then somehow, inexplicably, one of my charges escapes."

"But he dies before he can tell anyone anything."

"Yes, but how can I be sure of that? Maybe he lived long enough to say something, and the cops are keeping that to themselves while they search for me. And, unbeknownst to them, they've come close a few times. My minions and I have had to adapt to avoid the helicopters with infrared. My pilot has had to change his flight plans several times. Maybe we're low on supplies because of that. In any case, my profitable life of ease has suddenly become stressful. So now…"

"You're looking for someone to blame."

"Precisely. And because I'm under stress, I'm not thinking logically. So, I pick on the guy who found Jacob's body. He's named in the newspaper. I do a little of my own research and discover, whaddya know, the dude is gay. Openly, marriedly, happily, walking aroundedly g-a-y. And, since I'm probably a self-loathing closet case, because who else would run a conversion camp, I decide to take out my frustrations about that and my loss of business on him."

"But you—he—must have confederates in town who are carrying out the harassment."

"Oh, sure. He'll keep a couple of layers of plausible deniability between him and the minions. Hell, he may not even be in New Mexico, but directing from elsewhere."

"So when they find the camp, the harassment may not stop."

"I think it will. Because when they find the camp, I predict that our dude will have already cut bait and run for the border."

"I hope you're right." Something occurred to me. "You wrote off December, but that visit was different, too. That's when we found Danny Norman."

"We being you and Ammo."

"Well, Chris and Meredith were there. But it was mostly Ammo."

"So you're the guy who finds the bodies. You and your dog."

I froze, staring at Jon. He turned and looked at me over the rims of his shades. I whispered, "They can't be connected."

"Probably not." He pushed his shades up and crossed his hands over his stomach. "Always preferable to keep an open mind, though, isn't it?"

I sat there, stunned, my thoughts whirling. Danny Norman had been investigating a pharmaceutical salesman turned drug dealer named Jason Poe, who'd poisoned Danny with a long-acting, obscure toxin that he would have had to order from Europe. At least, that's what the FBI concluded. They'd found no solid evidence that Poe was the perpetrator. Poe had turned himself in and denied everything under questioning, then walked to his van in the parking lot of the Alamogordo Police Department and shot himself in the head, thereby closing the case.

I ran through everything I knew about both cases in my mind. There were no points of overlap.

Other than me.

I said out loud, "Sometimes a coincidence is just a coincidence."

Jon said, "Sometimes."

I looked past him at Pete and Liz; she was talking softly to him. That was good, except that Pete had nearly drained the bottle of Glenmorangie. It had only been about half full, but still…

I stood up. "We all need to eat something before we pass out."

Jon said, "Agreed."

I whipped up eight grilled cheese sandwiches—one of Pete's favorites—and carried them to the porch. Liz took two for herself and two for Jon and moved to the seat beside him.

I sat beside Pete and handed him a plate. "Eat up."

"Mm. I'm hungry." He took a big bite of a sandwich. "Yummmmm."

"Pretty damn good, if I do say so myself." I took a moment to observe Pete and decided that he was well on his way to drunk. "What were you and Liz talking about?"

"Prejudice. How different it is in Hawaii than here."

"She's told me that in Hawaii, what prejudice there is, is typically aimed at whites."

"Yeah. Over there, she never gets a second look. And she doesn't often in LA. But she said that when she and Jon are in Irvine, out and about, she gets the occasional stink eye."

I finished the first half of a sandwich and picked up another. "She's also said that when she's out with Jon, she gets glared at by Asian guys sometimes."

"Yeah, she mentioned that." Pete shook his head slowly. "We'll never get past this."

"What? Prejudice?"

"Yes. Racism. Classism. All the isms and phobias. They'll never end. Humans aren't capable of better."

"That's a depressing thought."

"It's realistic."

I poked him in the arm. "Hey. Realism is my turf."

He snorted. "About time I joined you there, don't you think?"

"I wish you didn't have to."

"Me, too." Pete drained the last of the whiskey into his glass and drank it. "Meeee, too."

The tire dealer called about a half hour after we'd finished eating. Jon drove me to town in Liz's car, then followed me home.

When we got back to the house, Pete and Liz had gone inside. I pulled into the garage and cut the ignition.

Jon parked behind me and joined me in the garage. I said, "What do we do now?"

"I don't know about you…" Jon stretched. "But I'm gonna have a phone conversation with your brother."

"Better do that out of earshot of Pete."

"Oh, yeah. I'll be in my room." He went into the house.

I lowered the garage door and followed him through the laundry room, then turned left toward my own bedroom. I found Pete sprawled face down on the bed, out cold.

For the best, I supposed. I'd never known Pete to throw up after a bender, but if he did, at least he was face down. I closed the door softly and went to find Liz.

She was on the back porch with Ammo, scrolling on her phone. She set it on the table beside her when she saw me. "All okay?"

"Yep, eight hundred bucks later."

"You sure you don't want to file insurance?"

"Pete said no. I guess he's thinking that it would just drag out the process. Knowing him, he wants to put it out of his mind if possible. Which is why he drank half a bottle of Glenmorangie."

Liz gave me a sideways look. "Do you think he can put it out of his mind?"

"Nope."

"What are you gonna do?"

I sighed deeply. Suddenly, I was mentally exhausted. "Long term? No idea."

"Short term, we're gonna demonstrate our shooting prowess to the locals, right?"

"Yeah. Immediate term?" I stood up. "I'm gonna drink another beer. Then you and I are gonna do some research."

Working together, it took Liz and I about an hour and a half to uncover the founding date of every church in Otero County. There were two that had only existed since 2017. One was a Spanish-language church down south of Orogrande, about 45 miles from Alamogordo.

The other was the Holiness church on Indian Wells Road.

I sent the information to Brian with a synopsis of Jon's theory. Maybe he could find a way to apply pressure there.

I reheated leftover chicken and dumplings for dinner. Pete roused himself to eat, then swallowed two Advil, donned his sunglasses, and joined the rest of us on the front porch.

There were thunderheads over the Organ Mountains, beyond White Sands, which probably wouldn't make it to us. But there was a steady breeze, kicking up the occasional dust devil at the back of our lot across the street.

We didn't say much. I couldn't even tell that Pete was awake, except that he moved occasionally. Jon was humming softly to himself; I couldn't make out the tune. Liz sat on the porch floor by the steps, cross-legged, eyes closed, facing west. From her breathing pattern, I figured she was meditating.

It grew dark. My thoughts and emotions had been swirling; now I tried to still myself and listen. Other than the occasional car on the next street over, there was little human sound. I could hear critters scurrying in the dark. Ammo could too, apparently; his ears were perked, and his nose was twitching, sampling the air.

Street lights began to come on, and I could see pinpricks of light in the distance that represented people's living rooms or kitchens. Over the mountains, the storm clouds were producing a lightning show. Every ten minutes or so, I could hear a faint rumble of thunder.

Finally, Liz opened her eyes and stood up. "I'm ready for bed, guys."

We all murmured assent. I locked the front door, checked all the windows, and armed the security system. Jon and Liz said goodnight and went to their room. I found Pete in the kitchen, drinking a glass of water, and hugged him from the side. "How's your head?"

"Better."

"Good. I'll take Ammo out, then come to bed."

He nodded. "I'm not very sleepy."

"You had that long nap."

"Yeah. I think I'll read in the office for a while."

"Okay." I kissed him and got the flashlight from the kitchen counter. "Ammo, come."

Ammo did his business, sniffed around for a few minutes, then trotted back to me. As we turned to go inside, one of the new motion-activated floodlights at the back of the property lit up.

Ammo growled. I whispered, "What's out there, buddy?"

I listened and heard scurrying animal feet. A coyote, most likely. After a minute, the light switched off.

Pete was in the office, deep into his criminal justice textbook. I kissed him goodnight, brushed my teeth, stripped, and collapsed into bed. Ammo circled three times on his own bed; I was asleep by the time he finished.

I didn't know how much time had passed. I wasn't sure that I was awake. Ammo was whining and snuffling at the closed bathroom door.

Why was the door closed? We left it open at night.

To my left, the clock said that it was 1:24. To my right, Pete was missing.

I sat up. Ammo, hearing me, turned and emitted a low moaning sound that I'd never heard from him before. Almost like he was mooing. Then he turned back to the bathroom door and started whining again.

Shit. I scrambled to get out of bed on Pete's side, got my legs tangled in sheets, and nearly landed on my head. Once I was upright, I took a deep breath, fear at what I might find flooding me, and slid the door open.

Pete was sitting on the floor, hugging his knees to his chest, sobbing.

Ammo got to him first, shoved his snout over Pete's right arm, and started to lick his face. Pete roused and pushed at the dog ineffectually. "Ammo. Cut it out."

I grabbed a towel from the rack to sit on, so I wouldn't freeze my naked ass on the cold tile floor and dropped down at Pete's left. "Oh, honey, what is it?"

"Everything. *Everything*."

I slid my right arm through his left and held on. "You scared the shit out of me. I didn't know what I was gonna find in here."

That brought his head up. He turned to me, his face wet. I realized that the sleeve of his t-shirt was wet, too, where he'd been wiping his eyes. "I wouldn't. I would never."

"Promise me."

"I promise." He reached for a box of tissues, which were under Ammo, and blew his nose.

"How long have you been in here?"

"I don't know. A while."

I hugged his arm. "It's been a rocky few weeks."

"No shit." He rested the side of his head against mine for a minute. "How do you do it?"

"Do what?"

He gestured with his right hand, which was still holding a tissue. "How do you deal with everything the way that you do? Yes, you get furiously angry, but it never shuts you down. I can see it in your eyes… you're always plotting, or sifting options. All this shit just makes my brain collapse. Yours goes into overdrive. How do you do that?"

I considered that for a moment. "When we were little, if one of us came home crying, or mad, or complaining about something, Sarge—or Dad—let us cry or vent for a few minutes. Then they'd ask, 'What are you gonna do about it?' 'I don't know' was unacceptable. 'What can I do?' resulted in, 'Let's think about this. What *can* you do?' And it was up to us to develop a plan of action. With input from the grownups, of course. Beating someone up wasn't an option."

Pete huffed a half-laugh, half-sob. I said, "Jeff, Kevin, and I were trained by the Marines, from near-infancy, to solve problems. I suppose it affected the wiring of our developing brains. And we all ended up in problem-solving professions." I nudged him. "Someone should conduct a case study on us."

He snorted and wiped his eyes on his already sodden shirt sleeve. "Yeah. Someone should."

I got up, soaked a washcloth in cold water, and wrung it out. Pete stretched his legs out; Ammo lay down and rested his head on Pete's right thigh. I sat back down on my towel and handed him the cloth. "Try this."

He buried his face in the cloth for a moment, then patted his eyes with it. "Thank you."

"You're welcome."

"What are we gonna do, Jamie?"

"I don't know."

He spluttered. "I thought that was unacceptable."

"It is. Made you laugh, didn't I?"

"Yeah." He patted his swollen eyes again. "I'm serious. What are we gonna do?"

I said, "I have faith in the cops. They'll eventually figure out who's doing this. Brian is even going to call the FBI tomorrow for an informal discussion. Once they find 'em, we'll press all the charges available to us."

"What do we do until then?"

"We have the security system now. I feel safe in the house. We haven't finished your to-do list, have we? Let's take a few more days and finish it. You'll feel better after accomplishing more tangible stuff, right?"

He sniffed. "Right."

"If we have to go someplace, we go together. And Jon's right, it's an open carry state. You can pack heat if you want."

He twisted the cloth in his hands. "What about our anniversary?"

Our fourth wedding anniversary--and Pete's forty-fourth birthday--was on July 3rd, one week from today. We'd planned to leave the weekend after, on the 7th. I said, "Do you want to spend it here?"

"I did. Before today. Do you want to spend it here?"

"Not particularly. Let's do this. We'll go home with Liz and Jon on Monday. That'll give us a day to decompress. I'll ask Kristen to bake a carrot cake for us." Carrot cake was Pete's favorite; we'd had one as our wedding cake.

He held the washcloth against his face for a minute. "Okay."

"And hey, if we change our minds tomorrow, we can go home tomorrow."

"Yeah." He sighed deeply and leaned his head back against the wall. "Damn it."

"Yup." I hugged his left arm again. "Think you can sleep now?"

"Maybe." He looked me up and down, noting my lack of clothing for the first time. "Aren't you cold?"

"Kinda." I stood up and held out my hand to him.

He grasped it, and I hauled him to his feet. He scratched Ammo's ears then trailed after me to the bedroom. I pulled a dry t-shirt from his drawer and tossed it to him, then dug out pajama pants for myself. I *was* cold.

Pete settled into bed, lying on his back, staring at the ceiling. I climbed in beside him and reached over to hold his hand. "Count sheep."

"What?"

"Seriously. Try it."

"One. Two. Three…"

"Silently."

He huffed a laugh. "Fine."

It didn't take long until his breathing evened out and he was asleep. It took me a while longer. I replayed our conversation in my head, wondering if there was anything else I could say to help him.

By the time I dozed off, I hadn't had any bright ideas.

Chapter 26

Thursday, June 27

I woke the next morning to the scent of bacon. I got up to pee, intending to rejoin Pete in bed, but he came into the bathroom as I was washing my hands. I said, "Hey, Sweet Pete."

"Hey." He wrapped his arms around me from behind and rested his chin on my shoulder. "I love you so much."

"I love you so much too. How do you feel?"

He took a deep breath. "Better. Everything looks better in the morning, right?"

"Sure. So does bacon."

He huffed a laugh and moved to the commode for his own peeing needs.

When we got to the kitchen, Jon was making pancakes and frying bacon. He waved the spatula at us. "Can I just tell you how much I adore this stove?"

Pete said, "I do, too. You should buy one."

Liz was at the table, reading the newspaper. She said, "Only when we have a real house."

I asked, "When will that happen?"

"Good question. We're not ready yet."

We stuffed ourselves—Jon's pancakes were fantastic—then decided to go sledding at White Sands. Just the thing to temporarily wipe our troubles from our minds. Jon drove; I noticed that he watched the rear-view mirrors closely. Once Pete and Liz were sorting out sled rental at the visitor center, I moved next to Jon and murmured, "Anything in the rear view?"

He smiled. "Nope. We're good."

When we got home at about noon, we were all hungry. We made sandwiches for lunch, then Liz and I hit the showers in preparation for our date at the shooting range. Once I was clean, I dressed in a form-fitting rugby jersey and my tightest pair of jeans. I slipped on a pair of deck shoes just as Pete came from the bathroom into the bedroom. "What the hell are you wearing?"

I spun to give him the full effect. “I’m encouraging erroneous expectations.”

“After Devin Maldonado worked so hard to make us sound ‘normal?’” He used air quotes around normal. “Besides. No one who’s been targeting us will be in this class.”

“Maybe not. But this is a small town. Word will spread.”

Liz had dressed down, in jeans and a black t-shirt. She and Jon both burst into laughter when they saw me. Jon said, “Role playing?”

“You betcha.”

“This will be *awesome*. I wanna go.”

Pete groaned. Liz said, “No way. What if one of them recognized you from *Two Days to Solve?*”

Jon grumbled but conceded the point.

Liz and I hopped into her car—an Acura MDX, the fanciest vehicle in our driveway—and headed for town. She was nearly gleeful with anticipation. “Suppose there will be any other women in the class?”

“Maybe. I just hope we’re not the only ones who signed up.”

Once in the parking lot of the range I strolled to the door leisurely. Liz walked beside me, trying not to laugh. A couple of other cars arrived; I heard the men that emerged from them greeting each other, then start muttering as they followed me to the door. I couldn’t hear everything they said, but the word *queer* was plain as day.

I smiled to myself.

The classroom was about a quarter full. Liz and I went straight for seats in the front row. I crossed my legs, which wasn’t the most comfortable position, but was the opposite of manspreading.

The instructor was at the front of the room, sorting handouts. He glanced up at me and raised an eyebrow, then went back to sorting. I heard people filter in behind me, then heard the murmurs. *Isn’t that...queer guys...pansy…*

I smirked. Beside me, Liz’s expression was fierce.

The instructor checked the time, then said, "All right, let's get started with introductions. I'm Andrew Banks." He pointed at me. "You next."

I said, "My name is Jamie Brodie. My husband and I are new in town, and we've been *harassed* and *threatened* ever since we moved here. I want to learn how to *defend* myself."

Liz was gazing serenely at the instructor. There were a few snickers from the back of the room, amused that the pansy thought that he could learn to handle a gun. Banks wasn't fazed. He pointed to Liz. "You next."

"I'm Liz Nguyen. I want to learn to shoot but my husband won't take me to the range until I pass this course."

The other attendees introduced themselves. I didn't recognize any of the names. Banks handed out the papers, which briefed us on New Mexico law, basic gun safety, and several other topics. He lectured for an hour and a half with PowerPoint slides then gave us a written exam, which Liz and I both passed with perfect scores.

Then we headed to the back of the building, to the shooting range.

I held back, acting as if I was reluctant, allowing the others to go ahead of me so that I could size up the competition. They were all even worse shots than I'd expected. Most of them only landed one round on the target at all. One of them managed to group all his shots within the 7—the widest circle—on the target's chest and was heartily cheered and high-fived by his comrades. No one came close to the X in the center.

It was Liz's turn. She allowed Banks to explain the gun to her, then assumed a perfect law enforcement shooting stance and landed all five of her shots in the 9 circle, the next ring out from the innermost ring.

The other students were muttering amongst themselves. Liz expertly ejected the clip and handed it and the gun back to Banks. "Thanks! This was *fun*."

Banks studied her for a second then inserted a new 5-shot clip into the Glock and turned to me. "Do you have experience with handguns?"

"Just a smidge."

"All right." Banks demonstrated the proper stance, then released the safety. "Aim for the center of the target."

"Yes, sir." The others clumped together to watch, a couple of them still nervously glancing sideways at Liz, but the rest openly smirking at the pansy who was afraid to handle the gun. I waited until Banks donned his ear protection, made sure from the corner of my eye that the others were watching, and fired.

My first four shots struck the target in the center of the chest, obliterating that X. I adjusted my aim and put the fifth and final bullet into the X right between the target's eyes.

Behind me, the rest of the group was silent, dumbstruck, staring at me open-mouthed. I removed my ear protection and ejected the clip. "Guess I aimed high on that last shot. Oops."

Banks looked back and forth between Liz and me. He asked softly, "Who *are* you two?"

Liz smiled sweetly. "I'm a cop's wife. And Jamie's best friend."

"And I'm an intensely angry gay man who's been shooting since he was four years old." I handed the clip and the gun to him. "What else do you want to know?"

The corner of Banks's mouth tipped up. "That oughta do it."

"One would hope." I grinned widely at the others, who still hadn't moved. "Tell all your friends."

Jon and Pete were on the front porch when we pulled into the driveway. Liz bounced out of the car with delight. "That was awesome! *We* were awesome."

Pete was shaking his head, but with amusement. Jon asked, "How'd you do?"

"Five shots inside the nine for me."

Jon beamed. "Thatta girl!"

I said, "Mine were all on the center X, except for the one in the middle of the forehead."

Pete said, "Showoff."

"That was the idea."

“How did they react?”

“Stunned silence.”

He barked a laugh. “Good. Not that it’ll make a difference.”

Jon said, “Hey, you never know. It might at least keep ‘em away from the house, if they know there’s a sharpshooter in residence.”

Pete sighed deeply. “I’d prefer that.”

Liz said, “As would we all.”

Chapter 27

Friday, June 28

The rest of our Thursday had been entirely unremarkable. We'd closed the front of the house and spent the remainder of the day on the back patio, eating and drinking and talking about Pete's pursuance of his master's degree. Jon, who'd majored in anthropology at UC Irvine, had been considering the same program.

Pete and I went to bed at the same time, for the first time in a while, and seized the opportunity to fool around. He dropped right off to sleep soon after. To my knowledge, he slept through the night...not that I was a reliable witness. I slept through, too.

The next morning at breakfast, we decided that we should take advantage of Jon and Liz's presence for the next three days, which we hoped would allow us to appear in town without incident. Ammo hadn't enjoyed an extended romp for a while, so Jon, Liz, and Pete decided to take him to the dog park, which was at the northern end of town. Jon and Pete both armed themselves before leaving.

I stayed home, partly to protect the house and partly to tidy up. I also secretly hoped that being with Jon and Liz would lift Pete's mood, possibly more than if I came along.

The indoor tidying didn't take long, so I went out back to see what needed to be done. Some of Pete's gardening tools were scattered around. I gathered them up and carried them to the garage, where they were currently stored, and made a mental note that we needed hooks for the greenhouse to hang stuff on.

Since Meredith's car was gone, I worked in that bay of the garage, opening its door to provide light and air. I dug the mill file out of our toolbox, cleaned the tools, and set to sharpening. Our shears, pruners, manual edger, and shovels soon all sported newly sharp surfaces. I sprayed each with WD-40 then hung them on their appropriate hooks.

I had my back to the door when I heard a soft noise—the scrape of a shoe. I turned to see a guy—shorter than me, but far bulkier, with a silver crew cut—standing in the driveway outside the open door.

He was carrying a baseball bat.

Oh, shit.

I was too far from the garage door opener button to push it. He stopped just at the doorway, the bat swinging from his right hand. "Where's the cocksucker?"

I reached behind my right shoulder to grab the shovel I'd just sharpened, not taking my eyes off the guy. "Who wants to know?"

He sneered, slapping the sweet spot of the bat in his left hand. "When I ask you a question, *asshole*, you'd better answer."

I said, "You're trespassing. Get the fuck off my property."

"So *you're* the cocksucker." He took a few steps closer to me, still slapping the bat in his hand, and nodded at the shovel. "Whaddya think you're gonna do with that? Knit me a sweater?"

Who the hell *was* this guy? I said, "I'll dig your grave with it, *asshole*."

The guy was fast. He suddenly swung the bat at my head. I managed to block the blow with the handle of the shovel and thanked the gods that we'd bought an all-steel shovel. A wooden handle would have snapped in two. I yelled, "What the fuck is your *problem?*"

The guy just grinned. He came at me like a Jedi knight with his lightsaber, raining blows. He was fast, but not particularly accurate. He didn't seem to have a strategy in mind, other than to try to back me into a corner. Unfortunately, he was succeeding.

He swung at my head. I blocked him and slashed down toward his torso. "*You motherfuckers tried to kill my dog!*"

He jumped back, momentarily distracted. "What? Didn't do nothin' to your fucking *dog*."

That confused me for a second, allowing the guy to smack me in the left shoulder—*ow*. I landed a decent blow with the flat side of the shovel on the knee, which made him howl.

He slugged me in the left thigh. I smashed him in the side of the head. "*Who sent you here?*"

He sneered. "Won't matter when you're *dead,* cocksucker."

The blow to the head didn't slow him down. The guy was a fucking Berserker. Completely crazed. I decided he must be on meth or something and realized that I'd better step up my game. I slashed at him with the sharpened end of the shovel, and opened a gash on his left arm, just above the elbow.

That made him even madder. But I was mad, too… now the bastard was bleeding all over my clean floor. I yelled, "You're gonna mop that up, motherfucker!"

He charged, backing me against the tool bench. I managed to duck and scramble to his other side so that the driveway was at my back now.

I don't know why I didn't run, or at least get into the street where someone might have seen us and called the cops. I was angry and fighting for my life and escape simply didn't occur to me. Whoever this guy was, I wanted to take him *down.*

Attack and parry. Attack and parry. I knew that eventually I'd start to tire, and I didn't think this asshole would. I didn't know whether it was meth or 'roid rage, but he was definitely on *something.* I thought of Pete, and my dad, and a new burst of furious energy surged through me.

I slashed him across the chest, slicing open his t-shirt. He slammed me in the right hip.

I went for his torso again and opened a gash across his ribs. He swung for my ribs and landed a glancing blow.

After what seemed like an eternity of blocking and swinging, I finally managed to smash him in the head again with the back of the shovel. He staggered to his right, temporarily lowering the bat, and I aimed for his head one more time.

I didn't mean to severely injure him. I only hoped to knock him unconscious. But my hands were sweating, and my grip slipped slightly on the handle of the shovel. I swung hard and hit the guy with the sharpened blade edge, right in the back of the neck.

The handle of the shovel transmitted the crunch of bone, and the guy went down like a sack of bricks, the baseball bat rolling out of his hand. I approached him and kicked the bat away. Blood was gushing from the wound; the shovel blade had sliced through the muscles of the left side of his neck.

Maybe I'd sliced his jugular. Had I *killed* him? *Shit.* I gripped the shovel in case I had to use it and approached him. "Hey. Asshole."

He rolled his eyes up at me. Alive, then. Still hanging on to the shovel, I made a wide berth around the guy toward the shelf where I'd left my phone, when my head exploded. Red, white, pain.

Black.

Hot metal against my face.

Pain.

The sound of an engine.

Black.

Being dragged by my feet.

Male voices. Accusing.

Hitting a hard surface.

Black.

I regained fuzzy consciousness. I couldn't see a thing...then realized that I was blindfolded. The pain in my head was more severe than any I'd ever experienced. I'd had two or three mild concussions on the rugby pitch, but *nothing* like this. My pulse pounding in my temples—throughout my entire head—was excruciating.

I tried to wiggle my fingers. The good news was that I succeeded. The bad news was that my hands were tied behind me.

A matched set with the blindfold, no doubt. And... I hadn't realized it until that moment, but I was gagged as well.

I was lying on my left side on a hard, rough surface. Concrete, I thought. The room I was in smelled of something sharp, acrid, singed.

I didn't move. My brain was foggy, but instinct kept me silent and still. I had no idea whether I was being guarded.

A door opened, and I sensed a bit of light seeping under the edges of my blindfold. A deeply pitched male voice said, "Is he alive?"

Footsteps approached. I could sense someone close to me. I tried to breathe shallowly. A different, higher, male voice said, "He's breathing."

Relief flooded Deep Voice's words. "*Good.*"

Good? I'd figured they intended to kill me. Maybe not...

"Why the *fuck* did you bring him up here?"

Deep Voice said, "I didn't know what the boss would want me to do, so I brought him. It gives us more time to get outta here."

High Voice said, "But now it's gonna slow us down to decide what to do with him."

"You heard the boss. We're not gonna do *anything* with him…"

The door opened again and someone else entered the room. Another male voice—familiar, somehow—said, "Is he alive?"

Deep Voice snarled. "You told us this guy was gay!"

"He is! He told me himself!"

What? Who the *fuck*...?

Where *was* I?

High Voice said, "Oh, yeah? Well, Mr. Light in His Loafers there nearly decapitated Jimmy with a fucking *shovel*. The guy's built like an eighteen-wheeler. I never saw any gay guy like *that*."

I couldn't decide whether the eighteen-wheeler crack was an insult or not. Jimmy must be the troll I fought with in the garage. Familiar Voice asked, "Will Jimmy be okay?"

Deep Voice said, "He was bleeding out on the floor when I left him. Do you call that *okay?*"

Familiar Voice yelped, "You *left him there?*"

"Yes, I left him there. What would you suggest? That I drag his body up here? Loading Shovel Boy in the truck was dangerous enough in broad daylight. If I'd taken the time to haul Jimmy, too, someone surely would have seen me."

High Voice said, "Fuck Jimmy. He'll never rape another kid. That's okay with *me*."

Whoa. Wait.

Raping kids…

Could this be the *conversion camp?* If so, then was Jimmy the *rapist?*

And I'd nearly *decapitated* him?

Outstanding.

But why had *he* come after me? Unless he'd planned to bring me up here…

Oh, shit.

Familiar Voice squeaked. "What do we do now?"

Why was this voice familiar??

High Voice said, "The boss says to shut down. Pack up and clear out tonight."

Familiar whined, "But what about the operation?"

Deep said, "It's over. Go back to your congregation."

Congregation?

"B-b-but…" Familiar was distraught. "What about my money?"

High barked a laugh. "Your *money?* You'd better hope the boss lets you *live*."

"Where are you two going?"

"California. The boss has a new gig. He's tired of this business, anyway, and so am I. The overhead's too high."

Familiar sounded like he was hyperventilating. "But I depend on this salary! My church can't support me!"

Church? My memory was waking up. I'd heard this voice...*where?*

Deep said, "Sounds like a personal problem."

"What about the boys?"

High said, "Boss says leave 'em here. They'll find their way out. Or not. Again, not our problem."

Familiar asked, "What about him?" Meaning me, I supposed.

Deep said, "Boss said to leave him, too."

Familiar said, "No. Let me hold him for ransom."

Deep and High laughed uproariously at that. Deep spluttered, "*You?* Seriously?"

"*Yes.*" Familiar sounded stubborn. "That fancy house he lives in cost big money. There must be more where that came from. Let me collect some of that, and I'll disappear to Mexico. You'll never have to worry about what I might say to the police."

Whoever this clown was, he knew where I lived. Someone from Alamogordo…

A moment of silence from the others. Then Deep said slowly, "That smacks of blackmail."

Familiar said, "Not blackmail. Just a friendly business arrangement."

High said, "Yeah, right. Then what? You let this guy go? He knows who you *are*. He knows where you *work*. You won't make it to El Paso, much *less* Mexico, before the cops catch up to you."

Deep said, "Not to mention, you're the *only* one of us that Shovel Boy can identify. All you are anymore is a liability."

I could identify him? Okay, obviously, since I'd apparently told this person myself that I was gay…

I heard a snapping sound. Familiar squeaked again. "What the hell are you doing? No! Forget what I said! I'll come with you. I'll…" His words ended in a choking gurgle, and something extremely heavy hit the floor with a solid *thud.*

High said, "So long, Todd, ya fat bastard."

Todd. The pieces of my memory finally fused. Pastor Todd Jackson, from the church on the corner of Ocotillo and Scenic, right down the street from our house. He'd come to the house last December…

He was involved in the conversion camp?

Holy fucking shit.

Deep snorted. "Should we leave him here?"

"We don't have time for anything else. Baxter will be here as soon as it's dark. We've gotta clean out the office."

"Where do we leave Shovel Boy?"

Another moment of silence while they considered. High said, "I'm thinkin' we should torch this building. We need to get rid of Jimmy's equipment and DNA, and that's the fastest way. We'll leave Todd in here, so it'll take 'em longer to identify him."

Damn, damn, damn. Deep said, "And this guy?"

"We'll drag him outside, well away from the building. We'll light the fire right before we take off. Someone'll see it eventually and find the kids. If they find this guy too, it's no skin off our nose. If they don't find him before the cougars and coyotes do…"

"Another personal problem."

High laughed. "Okay. Let's clear out the office first."

"Right. Bring all the paperwork in here, start the fire with it."

"Good idea. I'll haul the files over here, you stow the computers."

"Yeah. Then we…"

A male voice that I'd recognize under any circumstances said cheerily, "*Then* we blow your fuckin' heads off!"

Another vaguely familiar voice, this one female, snapped, "FBI! Hands behind your heads! Out in the hallway! *Now!*"

I heard pounding footsteps and the sounds made by a gathering army. In this case, I figured, SWAT or a similar tactical force. Someone knelt beside me and ungagged me, then lifted the blindfold. I looked up into Jon's eyes. He said, "Hi there."

I attempted to speak, but my mouth was so dry it was nearly impossible. Jon sliced through the zip ties on my hands and ankles and helped me sit up...which forced me to grab my head before it fell off. I groaned.

Someone else bent over me. Brian Cochrane, who handed me a bottle of water and gingerly explored the back of my head with his fingers. I flinched away from him. "Ow."

"Sorry."

I chugged water until I thought I could form words. "There are kids here somewhere."

"We found 'em." Brian straightened up. "All alive but battered. Medical choppers are on their way."

"Where are we?"

"At the head of Masterson Canyon."

That didn't tell me much. I asked Jon, "What are you doing here?"

Before he could answer, a ruckus erupted in the hallway. I couldn't see what was going on. A male voice yelled, "Knife!" just as the female voice yelped in pain. Running feet, then a burst of gunfire, then multiple voices shouting.

Brian shouted, "What's going on?"

A guy I recognized from somewhere—my brain was barely functioning—stuck his head through the door. "Meeker's been slashed. The suspects made a run for it. We stopped 'em."

With bullets, I supposed. I sighed. Jon said, "Me coming along was the only way we could convince Pete to stay home."

Oh, poor Pete. Frantic wouldn't begin to describe his state. I said, "I don't have my phone."

Brian said, "It wouldn't matter if you did. There's no service up here. We'll use the landline here to call."

I said, "Maybe you should do that now."

Brian chuckled. "On it."

I turned my head to the left, verrrry slowly. There were two rooms, doors closed, both with large plate glass windows. There were heavy drapes drawn across the windows from the outside. To my right were several rows of folding metal chairs, with a center aisle leading to a wooden lectern.

Straight ahead of me, Todd Jackson's body was sprawled on its back in a pool of blood. His throat was cut.

Jon helped me to my feet, which brought a wave of dizziness crashing over me. He propped me against the wall. "Drink more water."

As I tipped my bottle up, I heard the welcome sound of helicopters.

I wasn't allowed to enjoy my first helicopter ride. The flight paramedic kept shining lights in my eyes, taking my blood pressure, and asking me questions. Against the other side of the chopper, two flight nurses were having trouble finding a vein for an IV on a skinny kid who looked like he might be sixteen. He was crying softly.

At the hospital, I was hustled right from the helicopter to the ER. The nurses repeated all the tests the paramedic had done and gave me a shot of something, then I was whisked off to the MRI scanner. When I was brought back to my ER cubicle, Pete and Steve were there.

Pete had been crying. When he saw me, he started again. I reached my free hand—the one that wasn't tied to an IV—out to him. "Pete. Hey. I'm fine."

He grabbed my hand like it was a lifeline. "You're covered in blood, and your face is a bruised mess."

"Not my fault."

Steve snorted. A stocky white guy in scrubs who I hadn't seen before—at least, not that I remembered—pushed through the curtain into the cubicle. "Mr. Brodie?"

"Yo, dude." Whatever was in that shot they'd given me, it seemed to be working.

"I'm Dr. Adams." He stopped at my right side. "How many fingers am I holding up?"

"Three."

"Now?"

"One."

"Now?"

"Four."

"Good. Follow my finger with your eyes."

I followed. He said, "Good. Touch my finger, then touch your nose."

I complied.

"Good." He pulled a penlight from his pocket and flashed it in my eyes again. "What day is it?"

I sighed. "It was Friday, last I looked."

The corner of his mouth tipped up. “Who’s the president?”

“A reality TV star with the emotional control of a two-year-old.”

Dr. Adams smirked. “Okay. Have you ever had a concussion before?”

“Twice. Once in middle school, once in college. I played rugby.”

“Ah.” He rolled a stool to the bedside and sat. “Your MRI was perfectly normal. No sign of bleeding on the brain at all. I want to admit you to the ER overnight for observation. We’ll get your head stitched up. Any nausea?”

“No. I’m *hungry*.”

“Okay, we’ll see what we can rustle up for you to eat.” He pushed the stool away as he stood and spoke to Pete. “You’re his husband?”

Pete snuffled. “Yes. Can I stay with him?”

“Sure.” Dr. Adams looked around the narrow room. “We’ll...um...figure something out.” He grabbed my right foot and gave it a friendly shake. “A neurologist will be in to see you soon, and we’ll find something to eat for you.”

“Thanks.”

A nurse appeared in a moment, bearing a cup of chocolate ice cream with a wooden spoon. “I’m afraid the hospital kitchen is closed already. But your family is welcome to bring something in for you.”

I pointed at Steve. “Your job. Lo mein or something like it.”

“Yes, sir.” He saluted and left.

The nurses stitched up my head then dragged in a recliner for Pete, who struggled to stay awake with me but couldn’t manage it. By the time my dinner arrived—pad thai, delivered by Liz—he’d succumbed to exhaustion.

I accepted the steaming carton and the set of chopsticks. “Where’d you get this?”

Liz perched on the rolling stool beside my gurney. “There’s a Thai place downtown. I’m surprised you haven’t found it yet.”

"Huh." I sucked down a mouthful of noodles. "Oh, man. I'm starving."

"How's your head?"

"Numb, at the moment. They gave me a shot of something. Where's Jon?"

"At your house, on the phone with Kevin." Liz yawned. "He'll pick me up in a bit. Steve dropped me off here. I like him."

"Yeah, Steve's cool." I shoveled in more noodles.

"Do you want to hear about the case?"

"Um." I blinked at her. "Use small words."

She frowned. "Does it hurt to think?"

"No. I'm just...fuzzy."

"Okay. There were about twenty kids at the camp. Most of them in their late teens, and enough of them underage to build a slam dunk case, if they ever find anyone to build it against. They're from all over the country."

"Are they okay?"

She grimaced. "Most of them will be, at least physically. They brought the least injured ones here. The others were flown to Albuquerque and El Paso."

"What about the guy I hit with the shovel?"

Liz eyed me. "I don't know if I'm supposed to tell you."

"Oh, come on. I can take it."

"I hope so. He died in the ambulance on the way to the hospital." She leaned in, watching me closely. "How do you feel about that?"

I froze, chopsticks midair, noodles dangling. "He was alive when I left him."

"Yes, he was. Barely."

"He's… I killed him."

"You were fighting for your life."

I killed someone. "I overheard—he was the one raping those kids."

"Fucking *bastard*. You performed a public service. That's how you should choose to interpret it."

I scraped the bottom of the carton, drawing more noodles toward its mouth. “I can’t process this.”

Liz winced. “I shouldn’t have told you.”

“Yes, you should. It’s just…” I couldn’t explain the swirl of emotions in my clouded brain. “*Shit.*”

“He was an ex-cop.”

“What?”

“A sheriff’s deputy in Lincoln County, who got fired when he was convicted of raping a twelve-year-old and possessing meth. The Alamogordo cops who responded to your garage recognized him.” Liz looked around stealthily and lowered her voice to a whisper. “They didn’t rush to call an ambulance.”

“How’d he ever get out of jail?”

“That I don’t know.”

I finished the pad thai and set the carton aside. “You think Pete’s asleep?”

Liz glanced at Pete, who hadn’t even twitched when I said his name. “Out cold. Why?”

I whispered anyway. “I don’t know if I can ever live here full time.”

She regarded me, one eyebrow cocked. “You don’t have to live here full time. Even if...when...you leave the library, you can live half-time in Santa Monica. Keep your California residency. Or, you know, sell the house, stay at the library, and don’t live here at all.”

I closed my eyes. My head was starting to hurt again, and the overhead light was too bright. “I don’t know if Pete would agree to that.”

“Well, you’ll have to discuss it, won’t you?”

A nurse came in, Jon behind her. She checked my monitors and asked, “How do you feel?”

“My head’s starting to throb again.”

“Okay. I’ll see if it’s time for another shot yet.” She bustled out.

Jon said, “How many stitches?”

“Twelve.”

"Yikes." He nodded at Pete. "I see he was finally able to relax."

"Jon. I killed someone."

His tone was gentle. "We'll think about that tomorrow."

"Did you tell Kevin?"

"Yeah. He was gonna call your dad."

At the mention of my dad, a powerful wave of homesickness washed over me. I said, "I wanna go *home*. Can we go home tomorrow?"

Liz squeezed my forearm. "We'll let you sleep. We can talk about all of this tomorrow."

Chapter 28

Saturday, June 29

I didn't sleep. The neurologist arrived shortly after Liz and Jon left, and repeated all the testing that Dr. Adams had done. She asked for more detail about my previous concussions, then told me I'd probably be fine and wrote me a prescription for painkillers. Once she was gone, I nearly dozed off, but then a nurse came in to check on me. And every hour thereafter. I understood that was the point of observation, but by the time morning came I was cranky. And hungry again. Pete didn't wake up until a nurse brought me a breakfast tray. I lifted the lid, and the scent of bacon wafted through the room.

Pete roused, sniffing the air. "Bacon."

"You want it?"

He blinked at me, seemingly remembering where he was and why we were here. "Oh. No, you eat. How are you?"

"Grumpy and exhausted. Approach with caution."

He stood and stretched, then snagged a slice of bacon from my tray. "Just one piece."

I tasted the scrambled egg then searched the tray for the salt and pepper packets. "They kept waking me up to test my pupils."

"How's your head feel?"

"Achy throbbing. Throbby aching."

"Are you still fuzzy?"

"Not as much." I did seem to have more focus this morning, despite my sleepless night.

"They should discharge you this morning."

"They'd *better*."

They did. The neurologist came in as I was drinking the milk that accompanied my meal. She performed a thorough exam and declared me fit to be released. A nurse removed my IV and brought me a long list of signs and symptoms to watch for, and I was freed.

To my surprise, a reporter, accompanied by a cameraman, was waiting for us outside the ER entrance. "Mr. Brodie? I'm Scott Torres from KALC in Las Cruces. Could we have a few minutes of your time?"

Pete began to refuse, but I held up a finger to stop him. "I can't tell you much."

"How are you feeling?"

"Lousy."

"What did you see at the camp?"

"Very little. I was blindfolded."

"Has your experience impacted your impression of Alamogordo?"

I felt a wave of anger start to crest. "Do you really want to know?"

The reporter looked surprised. "Well, yeah."

I crossed my arms. I'd been dwelling on this all night, and I boiled over with it. "When my husband and I decided to build a second home, we chose Alamogordo for several reasons. We had family here. We wanted to live in a place where we could see the stars at night. We wanted to live in a place with a small-town atmosphere, where neighbors said hello in the grocery store and helped each other out in times of trouble. We wanted to live in a place where we could contribute to the community in some way. So we built here. We made sure to hire local workers and contractors. We dropped a *major* chunk of change into the economy of this town. And then what happens when we move in? We *immediately* start receiving threats, informing us in no uncertain terms that gays are not welcome here. Our property is damaged. Someone tries to *poison* our *dog*. And then, yesterday, someone tries to *kill* me in my own garage. After all that, how the hell do *you* think these experiences have impacted my impression of Alamogordo?"

The reporter said, "How have your neighbors responded?"

"*What* neighbors? Other than law enforcement, Joey Norman, and Ross Harris, no one in this town has done *shit* to help us or stand up for us. No one has come forward with *any* information about whoever has been perpetrating these attacks. I have *never* felt more unwelcome *anywhere* at any time in my *life*. I wish I'd never *heard* of Alamogordo."

Pete was standing off to the side, wringing his hands with anxiety. The reporter said, "What are your plans?"

"Right now, I plan to go home and take some aspirin. After that, all bets are off." I turned and walked away.

Our CR-V—I did a double take at the sight of the new tires; I'd forgotten—was in the ER visitor lot. I climbed in without speaking. Pete shot a worried glance at me as he started the car but didn't say anything.

An Alamogordo PD cruiser was parked at the entrance to our street. I didn't recognize the officer who climbed out and stopped us. He walked to my side of the car, so I rolled down the window.

He leaned in. "Mr. Brodie. I'm Officer Brock. How are you?"

"Alive and mostly well, thanks."

He nodded. "You take care, now." He backed the patrol car up so that we could pass. When we pulled into our driveway, I saw that he'd blocked the street with his car again.

Pete lifted his hand to push the garage door button, and I reached out to stop him. "Don't."

He studied me but didn't argue. "Okay."

We entered the house through the front door. The FBI was waiting for me at the kitchen table. Two agents, one the handsome, dark-haired man that I'd recognized in the hallway; one an intense, red-headed woman. Mulder and Scully.

I didn't remember their names. I did recall that they were assigned to the Las Cruces FBI office. The last time I'd seen them, they were questioning Pete, Steve, and me after we'd stumbled across several fragments of Dixon Gill's hot air balloon in the scrub south of town.

Scully's left forearm was wrapped in a pressure bandage, clean white gauze peeking out from one end. She said, "Mr. Brodie. Special Agent Meeker and Special Agent Armistead. We'd like to ask a few questions."

I said, "I'm not saying *anything* before I take a shower. I bet *you've* had one."

Armistead tried to hide his grin. Meeker scowled, but I saw her realize that, in my case, a filthy witness was a hostile witness. "Make it fast."

"Yes, ma'am."

In our bathroom, Pete helped me out of my clothes. He showed me the t-shirt I'd been wearing; the back was soaked in blood. "Can I toss this?"

"Please do."

He dropped it into the wastebasket, then turned back to me and blew out a breath. "Oh, hon. You're bruised and scratched all over."

"I doubt that my kidnappers treated me gently."

We both scrubbed down, Pete helping me to avoid wetting my stitches. I dressed in the loosest pair of sweatpants I could find and one of Pete's oversized t-shirts and padded to the kitchen, where Liz met me with two bottles, one of Coke and the other of my pain pills. I accepted them gratefully. "Where's Jon?"

She gave me a significant look. "Pressure washing the garage floor."

Ah. Cleaning up Jimmy's blood. And some of mine, too, I supposed. Liz said, "The agents are in the den."

I swallowed a pill and carried my Coke into the great room, where Meeker and Armistead were perched on one leg of the sectional sofa. I lowered myself into a recliner facing them. "How many stitches, Agent Meeker?"

She frowned at me warily. "Twenty-six."

"You win. I only needed twelve." I raised the footrest on the recliner and waved my Coke at them. "Ask away."

Meeker said, "Tell us how this started."

I related the events that took place in the garage. When I finished Armistead said, "You didn't see who hit you?"

"No. I thought Jimmy was alone until the moment my head exploded. What did he—whoever—hit me with?"

"A lug wrench." Armistead raised an eyebrow. "You're lucky to be alive."

"Yes, sir. I don't doubt that for a minute."

Meeker asked, "What happened next?"

"The next thing I remember was waking up in that room where you all found me." I repeated the conversation I'd heard between Deep, High, and Todd.

Meeker said, "Did the other two men refer to each other by names?"

"No, ma'am. Todd didn't call them by names either. They did mention someone named Baxter, who was supposed to arrive after dark."

Armistead said, "We found a narrow clearing on the other side of the ridge that seems to have been used as a runway. Maybe Baxter was a pilot."

I said, "Did he arrive?"

"No. We've had people on site since we found you yesterday. No one else showed up."

Meeker asked, "What did they say about a boss?"

I tried to remember. "The boss had instructed Deep and High to shut the operation down, that he was getting out of the business. Todd didn't like that and wanted to hold me for ransom. He threatened to talk to the cops if they didn't let him take me. That's when they killed him."

"Anything else about the boss?"

"Um...they said he had a new gig. They were supposed to clean out the office and go to California."

"Where in California?"

"They didn't say."

"What was the new gig?"

"They didn't say. Are Deep and High dead?"

"Yes." Meeker didn't look pleased. "We hope to identify them by fingerprints."

Armistead asked, "Is there anything else you can remember?"

"No. Sorry."

He stood and handed me a card. "If you do remember anything else, please call."

"I will."

Meeker said, "Get some rest."

"Yes, ma'am."

Pete was napping in our bedroom. I'd dozed off in the recliner when the doorbell rang. I vaguely heard Jon speak to someone at the door, then he came into the room. "Are you up for a visit from the mayor?"

I sighed. No doubt my interview had aired on TV by now. "Why not?"

Jon left the room then momentarily returned with a man of about sixty, wearing jeans, a plaid shirt, and cowboy boots, carrying a Stetson in his hands. He said, "Mr. Brodie, I'm Lee Poole, mayor of Alamogordo."

I knew it was petty. I didn't care. I said, "It's Dr. Brodie."

"Dr. Brodie. I'm sorry." Poole worried the brim of his hat with his hands. "Actually, I'm here to apologize for everything that's happened to you. This is not representative of our town."

I said, "You sure about that? 'Cause it feels pretty representative to me."

He flushed. "Dr. Brodie, 98% of the people in this town are the sort of neighbors you hoped to find. Anyway. On behalf of the city, I want to formally apologize, and welcome you to the town, and ask you to forgive us for everything that's happened. And we hope very much that you'll stay."

I lifted my hand from the arm of the recliner then let it drop again. I was *so* tired. "Apology accepted. We haven't yet discussed whether or not we'll stay."

The mayor handed me a business card. "My cell phone number is written on the back. You call me, any time of day or night, if you need *anything*."

"Thank you."

Jon saw him out then came back to the family room. "That's a start, huh?"

"I guess." I took stock of my physical condition and determined that I didn't feel too bad, as long as I didn't move. "What happened yesterday?"

He held up a finger. "I need refreshment for this discussion. Do you need anything?"

"A bottle of water, please."

"You got it." He went to the kitchen then returned with water for me and a beer for himself. "We didn't miss you by much. We arrived at the same time the cops did. Jimmy was still bleeding when we found him. Ammo was going nuts, so Liz dragged him inside. Pete was freaked and started searching for you in the house."

"Poor Pete."

"Yeah. He was a mess." Jon took a drink.

"Wait. The cops got here at the same time as you? Who called 911?"

"Your mail carrier. He was delivering on the next street over when he spotted a black pickup with a Texas tag parked by an empty lot. A man appeared from the direction of your street, which the mail carrier thought was weird, then jumped into the truck and drove off. The mail carrier finished his deliveries on that street, then drove over toward this street. He was about to turn left from Ocotillo when the same black truck came flying out of your street without stopping and turned west. The mailman drove onto this street, saw your open garage door, and checked to see what was going on. He thought you might have been burglarized. When he saw Jimmy, he called 911."

I sighed. "Finally. Someone saw something."

"Yep. We got lucky. Nice guy, your mailman. He said it only took the cops about three minutes to respond."

"I've never met him."

"You should write him a thank you letter. Anyway. Two of the cops seemed to know Pete. Smallwood and Garza?"

"Yeah. They responded to our previous calls."

"The other two recognized the guy on the floor. Jimmy Freeman. Said he was a former deputy in the next county over."

"Liz mentioned that. So he was still alive when they got there?"

"Barely. The EMTs started CPR once they arrived, but I'm sure he was dead by then."

"Where did he come from? I didn't realize he was there until he was standing in the doorway."

"From shoe prints, it looks like he walked from where the black truck was parked, through your property along the base of the wall, and came right around the corner to the garage. No way you could have seen him coming."

"Did the other guy carry me back through the yard?"

"No. He must have followed Jimmy to see what was happening, then whacked you on the head once Jimmy was down. I think he left you lying here while he drove his truck around and backed it up to the open garage bay, then tossed you into the truck bed. There was another pool of blood closer to the door that must have come from you, and blood drips in a trail from there to the garage opening."

"So they had the truck description...how'd they find the camp?"

"Jimmy's phone was in his pocket."

I chuckled. "Methinks Jimmy was a dumbass."

"No doubt. In his defense, he didn't expect to be the one bleeding out on the garage floor."

"GPS?"

"Nope. Texts to and from his meth dealer, who fortunately lives here in town and is known to the APD. They were thrilled to have hard evidence that he was dealing; they said he'd been hard to pin down. They snatched him up and convinced him to tell them where he met Jimmy for deals, which was the intersection of the canyon road with the trail to the camp. By that time Brian had pulled in the FBI, since you'd been kidnapped."

"Oh. I wondered why they were there, and not the sheriff."

"Apparently your sheriff is not pleased that he was shut out. But from what Brian said, they don't have the resources for an operation like this."

"Probably not. Is Brian in trouble?"

Jon scoffed. "Nope. His boss went with us. We met Meeker and Armistead and their team out on the bypass and headed into the mountains. FBI had scrambled a helicopter from Holloman—don't ask me how—and it spotted the truck heading south from Cloudcroft, down one of those little county roads. He was nearly an hour ahead of us, but he still had a way to go. The chopper followed him right to the camp, then described the layout of the place to us as we approached."

I smiled. "My tax dollars at work."

"Worth every penny." Jon stood and gave me a friendly swat on the leg. "Need anything?"

"If you promise to intercept any further visitors, I'll write you into my will."

He laughed. "Done."

By 7:00 that evening, I was wiped out. Pete came to the bedroom with me to supervise my preparations, then tucked me in. As he pulled the covers up over me, I said, "I want to go home."

He was quiet for a minute then said, "You're traumatized."

"Well, yeah. I killed someone, Pete. *In this house*."

He stroked my hair, wrapping curls around his fingers. "He would have killed you."

"I know. But still."

"You should call Dr. Bibbins on Monday for an appointment. Talk it out with her."

"I will."

He sighed deeply. "I should have pushed harder for moving to Scotland instead of New Mexico."

"No. I don't want to cave that easily. It's just… right now, I don't know *what* to think. I want to go home."

"Do you think Alamogordo can ever feel like home to you?"

"I don't know. Before this month, I thought it might. But there's a shitload of ugliness here, and the population isn't big enough to hide us from it."

He was quiet again then said, “Well. We don’t have to make long-term decisions tonight.”

“I *can’t* make long-term decisions tonight. I can barely think straight. All I seem to be able to do is *feel*.”

“That’s typical, post-concussion.”

“I know.”

He lifted my left hand and began to run his thumb back and forth over my wedding ring. “*I* can make a short-term decision, though. Let’s go home with Jon and Liz.”

“Are you sure?”

“Yes.”

“We’ll have to leave the Jeep here.”

“We can fly back and get it later.”

I sighed. “I hate this. I feel like I’m running away. I don’t want to run.”

“You’re not running. You’re withdrawing temporarily to lick your wounds, so you can return to fight another day.” He squeezed my hand. “Ask Dr. Bibbins to refer you to a neuropsychologist who specializes in head trauma.”

“I will. Are there any such creatures in Alamogordo?”

“No. The closest are in El Paso. And that fact is the best reason for us to go home.”

I sighed. “Okay.”

He leaned over and kissed the tip of my nose. “Go to sleep. We’ll talk more in the morning.”

Chapter 29

Sunday, June 30

When I woke up the next morning, sunlight was peeking through the mini-blinds in the bedroom window. I turned my phone over and was shocked to see that it was 10:15. I rolled to my side and groaned out loud as stiff muscles and bruising came in contact with the mattress. I sat up, legs dangling, and my head began to throb. I waited for a few minutes to allow the dizziness to resolve, and the throbbing in my head quieted down.

I washed my face and brushed my teeth then dressed in the same sweats and t-shirt I'd worn last evening. When I walked into the main part of the house, it was cool, dim and quiet. No one was around, but there were six gift baskets on the kitchen table: four of fruit and cheese, one of wine and chocolate, and one of seeds and gardening tools. I could only find one card; the wine and chocolate were from Russell and Mandy McCarthy.

The Sunday paper was on the table as well. The headline read, **Masterson Canyon Gay Conversion Camp Raped and Tortured Teenagers**. The byline was Devin Maldonado's. Just reading the headline made my head throb again, so I decided not to try the rest of the story.

I pulled a banana from one of the fruit baskets, got a Coke from the fridge, and went in search of my family. The back patio was empty. I found them when I opened the front door. Pete, Steve, Meredith, Jon, Liz, and—to my surprise—Kevin were arrayed on the front porch. Ammo was at Pete's feet; he scrambled to his paws and greeted me joyfully as I emerged from the house.

Kevin was sitting by Pete; he offered me his chair and perched on the top of the two steps from the porch to the ground. I said, "What are you doing here?"

"I flew in late last night to help Jon ensure that everything here is resolved to our satisfaction. We have a meeting scheduled with Brian Cochrane and your police chief and sheriff this afternoon."

I raised an eyebrow. "You seriously think the New Mexico cops will take kindly to being lectured by the LAPD?"

Jon said, "We've already discussed it with Brian, and he's on our wavelength. One of those fruit baskets in there is from the police chief and his wife, so we don't anticipate issues on his end either."

"I saw the basket from Russell and Mandy. Who sent the others?"

Pete said, "The gardening basket is from Ross and Dianne Harris. One of the fruit baskets is from the people at the end of our street on Ocotillo, one is from those people…" He pointed to a house one street over to the west. "One is from Joey and Patti Norman, and one is from your library."

Liz said, "Which I didn't know anything about, but of course I'm here, not there. Your speech on TV yesterday seems to have made an impression."

"Excellent. It was meant to." I leaned my head gingerly against the back of the rocking chair, then decided that was a bad idea. "Kev, how are both you and Jon able to be gone?"

"I'm only here for two days. Max and Jill are up for the next case." Kevin smiled at me. "I thought I might drive you and Ammo home in your CR-V. Then Pete can drive the Jeep."

"Oh. That'll work, I guess."

Pete started to say something when a car turned onto our street. Jon and Kevin were both wearing hoodies, and I saw both casually reach for their waistbands. Steve said, "You guys are *carrying?*"

Jon said, "*Fuck*, yeah."

The car looped around the cul-de-sac circle and stopped in front of our house. A pair of women got out, one in desert camo pants, work boots and a t-shirt, the other in cargo pants and a polo shirt. Both had short cropped hair and were solidly butch. The one in camo eyed Kevin and Jon warily, palms out, placating. "Don't shoot, fellas. We come in peace."

The other woman was carrying a picnic basket. "I'm Theresa Summers, and this is my wife, Starr Flannery."

We all stood while Pete made the introductions. Liz and Jon offered their seats to Theresa and Starr, who said, "Ryan Cotton told us about you a couple of weeks ago, and we'd already intended to stop by. When we saw you on the news yesterday, we figured we'd better see if we could help make things right."

I said, "Oh, you know Dr. Cotton?"

Theresa said, "Yup. Through the Episcopal church. Ryan and I are both members of the vestry there."

Starr said, "We sure wish we'd gotten here before anyone else did."

Pete said, "We're delighted that you're here now. Can I get you something to drink?"

Theresa said, "No, thanks. We didn't come to stay. But we weren't sure you'd feel comfortable being seen in public for the next few days, so we brought provisions." She'd set the picnic basket at her feet; now she handed it to me.

I lifted the lid and pulled back the red and white checked cloth lining the basket. There were muffins, cookies, a loaf of something that might be carrot bread, and a casserole dish and a pie plate both covered in foil. "Oh, wow, this looks fantastic. Thanks so much."

Starr said, "You're welcome. You are *entirely* welcome here. We wanted to make sure you know that. Theresa and I are *thrilled* that you've moved here."

Liz asked, "How did you come to live here?"

Starr said, "I was an AFOSI agent at Holloman before Russell McCarthy."

Aha. That's how she'd recognized that Kevin and Jon were armed. She continued, "Always thought I might like to retire here, 'cause you can't beat the scenery, but I wouldn't have if I hadn't met Theresa beforehand. This is a lousy place to be gay and single. But I'd transferred from Holloman to Vandenberg, and I met Theresa in California. We got married there in 2013. I worked for one more year, then we both retired and moved here."

Theresa said, "We immediately got involved in the Episcopal church here, and most of our friends are folks we've met there. If you fellas are so inclined, I expect you'd have the same experience."

I said, "I appreciate the invitation. We'll think about it."

Starr stood up. "We'll get out of your hair. Hope you're feeling better."

"Thanks. I am now."

Theresa smiled. Starr said, nodding at Jon, "I recognize you guys. *Two Days to Solve*, right? LAPD homicide?"

Kevin said, "Yes, ma'am."

"Ha! *Damn.* Todd Jackson and his church of losers fucked with the wrong gays, huh?"

Jon said, "And we're gonna make them *intensely* sorry."

The rest of the morning was punctuated by visits from various townspeople, all bearing gifts. We met several of the neighbors, from along Ocotillo and from further down Las Lomas. All of them assured us that they'd had no idea what was happening to us, that we were most welcome, and if we ever needed anything, to please contact them.

Most of them seemed sincere.

Officer Smallwood drove down our street twice, slowly circled the cul-de-sac, and waved but didn't stop.

At 1:00 Pete heated up the casserole Theresa and Starr had brought—chicken with wild rice and almonds, which was marvelous—and we ate. After lunch Jon and Kevin headed downtown to their law enforcement summit. Pete, Steve, Meredith and Liz returned to the front porch. Ammo and I retreated to the bedroom for a nap.

When I woke up, Ammo was gone. I went to the kitchen to find the others gathered around Liz's oversized laptop, watching something on the screen. Pete spotted me and moved aside to make room. "Jon just texted us. Live announcement from the police chief."

Chief Hines was at a microphone, Tobias Rice standing behind his right shoulder, Sheriff Gordon Wayne at his left. Brian Cochrane was lurking behind Tobias. Hines was saying, "This afternoon, the Alamogordo Police Department and the Otero County Sheriff's Department have made several arrests for misdemeanor offenses committed against two new residents of Alamogordo. These misdemeanor charges will have hate crime penalties applied on top of the imposed sentence. I want to make it *abundantly* clear that this sort of criminal activity *will not be tolerated* in Alamogordo. This city and its residents have been *disgraced* by the illegal activities of a few of its citizens." He leaned into the mic and lowered his voice. "Take note, Alamogordo. *I will not have this in my city*." He stepped back. "Sheriff?"

Gordon Wayne moved to the mic. He didn't look thrilled to be there, but he said, "Let me extend what Chief Hines said to Otero County. There is no place for hate crimes here." He backed away.

Hines gestured to Brian, who stepped to the mic. "Detective Brian Cochrane, New Mexico State Police. New Mexico thrives as a state because of its diversity. The State Police will not tolerate harassment of any citizen. Period."

Hines moved back into the spotlight. "If any of you have any information about crimes perpetrated against the residents of Las Lomas Court, come forward. *Now*." He nodded to whoever was manning the camera. "That's all."

Liz said, "I'm not sure the sheriff is sincere."

Steve snorted. "I'm gonna have a word with ol' Gordon next time I see him."

Jon and Kevin were back in time for dinner. We had a pan of lasagna from another neighbor, and Pete had used the apples from the fruit baskets—we'd ended up with six—to make a cobbler. Steve and Kevin washed dishes, then Steve and Meredith left.

We were on the back patio after dinner, finally getting a chance to relax, when the doorbell rang. Pete and I both groaned in unison. Kevin said, "I'll get it."

He came back in a moment with Brian Cochrane, who accepted a beer and flopped into an empty chair. "We got all of your vandals but one. Fingerprints identified some, the others got snitched on, and APD has arrested them all. They'll be arraigned tomorrow, but they've all confessed."

Pete asked, "Who were they?"

"The deacons of Todd Jackson's church. He'd instructed them to cleanse the sin from the neighborhood."

Kevin said, "They're charged with misdemeanors. There won't be much punishment."

"They'll get as much punishment as is allowed by law. They'll appear before the only female judge in the district, and I guarantee she'll throw the book at 'em. They'll all have hefty fines and community service, and a few will have thirty days' jail time. A couple of those will lose their jobs."

I said, "Sounds good to me. Who didn't you get?"

"The one who tried to poison your dog. Josh Smallwood thinks he knows who the guy is, but we don't have cause to get a warrant yet."

Pete asked, "Who does Smallwood think he is?"

"A guy up north of the city limits who APD suspects of running a dogfighting ring. Josh lives up that way too, and he and his wife do animal rescue. Josh was already on a mission to bring the guy down, so this will add fuel to that fire."

I said, "Smallwood patrolled this street at least twice today."

"Yeah. Josh is good people." Brian drained his beer. "One other item of note. Do you remember, from back in December, that Danny Norman had GPS coordinates written in his notebook?"

Pete said, "Yeah...and?"

"One of the coordinates marked the intersection of Masterson Canyon Road with the trail that led to the camp."

What? I said, "Whoa. Wait a minute. Danny Norman had marked the location of the *camp?* Why?"

Brian said, "It's the same spot where Jimmy's dealer told us that he met Jimmy to sell meth. Maybe Jimmy or his dealer, or someone else at the camp, was involved somehow with the scheme that Danny was investigating? Maybe it's just coincidence."

I looked at Jon, who raised an eyebrow. His words from Wednesday reverberated in my head. "*You're the guy who finds the bodies. You and your dog.*"

Back in December, Todd Jackson had visited us five days after I'd discovered Danny's body.

Kevin said, "We don't believe in coincidence." I wondered if Jon had mentioned his theory to Kevin and decided that he surely must have.

Brian snorted. "No. We do not. I checked the case file; according to his phone GPS records, Danny had never actually traveled to that spot."

I said, "That's… Wow."

"Yup."

Kevin asked, "Any ID on the guys at the camp?"

"Yeah. Phil Mills and Preston Dunn. No criminal record for either of them, but Mills had been a cop in Marfa, Texas, and Dunn had been a city employee in Pecos, Texas. They'd been fingerprinted for their previous jobs."

Jon said, "Was the black pickup truck registered to one of them?"

"Yeah, to Mills, at an address in El Paso. FBI has a team there but hasn't found anything useful yet. He apparently lived alone."

Meredith said, "So identifying them isn't going to help in locating their boss?"

Brian sighed deeply. "It's early days, but right now it doesn't look hopeful."

Brian said good night and headed home. Kevin and Jon walked him out and were gone for several minutes. When they came back, their expressions were grim. Pete said, "What?"

Kevin said, "We've been discussing this on and off all day. Here's the thing… Jimmy knew where to find you. The obvious explanation is that Pastor Todd told him where you lived. My concern is that Jimmy passed that information on before his welcome demise."

Liz grimaced. "What are the chances of that?"

Jon said, "We know that Jimmy was a rogue actor. You overheard Mills and Dunn say that the boss didn't want anyone killed. We're sure that one of them was Jimmy's accomplice, so that one knew where you lived, but they're both deceased as well. The question is, did Jimmy, Mills, or Dunn tell the boss who you were?"

I said, "The boss knew they had me. He told them to leave me behind."

"Right. But did he learn that after the fact, or did he know they were coming after you beforehand? Did he send them here?"

Kevin said, "It's entirely plausible that Jimmy was going to ask for forgiveness rather than permission after dealing with you. It's also entirely plausible that the boss gave them his blessing."

My brain wasn't so scrambled that I couldn't add two and two. "If their boss has my name and address in Alamogordo, it wouldn't take him long to find out where I live the rest of the time."

Jon said, "I don't know why he'd come after you now. If he wanted you dead, they'd have killed you at the camp. Besides, you don't know anything that could hurt him. The camp is defunct, and the boss has no idea that you even overheard Mills and Dunn discussing the new gig in California. And he—or she, but likely he—was apparently only too willing to shut down the camp. Let's hope that he doesn't take personally the demise of the camp and his employees there. If he doesn't, he'll probably leave you alone."

Pete said, "But we should be vigilant."

Jon said, "Yes."

Kevin said, "I've called Kristen and asked her to bring Sam to our place for tonight and tomorrow. Just until we all get home."

Pete's niece, Samantha, who was housesitting for us in Santa Monica. Pete said, "Shit. Chris will freak *out*."

Jon said, "No reason she has to know. It's only two days."

Kevin said, "You guys remember Joyce Fox and Emma Lamb?"

I said, "Sure." Joyce Fox was one of Kevin's LAPD Academy classmates, now a Santa Monica PD patrol officer. Emma Lamb was an SMPD homicide detective whom we'd met on a case involving Fox and another SMPD cop.

Kevin said, "I've unofficially asked Joyce and Emma to unofficially keep an eye on your house until further notice. They're happy to help."

I tried to stay awake longer, but the siren song of my bed was too strong. Pete followed me and leaned in the bathroom doorway while I brushed my teeth. He sighed deeply. "Feels like I've aged ten years in the past four weeks."

"No kidding." I pulled my t-shirt over my head and kicked off my sweatpants. "What are the odds, do you think, that this boss is likely to act?"

"Minimal. It's like Jon said. The guy's likely to realize that you can't identify him in any way."

I tugged on pajama pants. "Are you just trying to make me feel better?"

"No, but I hope that's a side effect."

"You realize that now you're keeping something from Christine. As Lieutenant Nelson Hopkins would say, the shoe is on the other foot."

Hopkins was a cliché-spouting Internal Affairs cop who'd screened Kevin and Jon for *Two Days to Solve*. Pete snorted. "I'll let Sam explain it. Eventually. Do you want me to pack everything?"

"Oh. *Shit*. How rattled is my brain that I forgot that we have to pack?" I moved toward the closet.

"No, no. You go to bed. I'll pack."

"You're sure?"

"Yes." He guided me to the bed.

"Don't wrinkle my clothes."

He laughed and kissed me. "Shut up and sleep."

So I did.

Chapter 30

Monday, July 1

The next morning, Pete woke me up at five. I found our suitcases and Ammo's toys packed and already loaded in the CR-V, along with Russell and Mandy's wine and chocolate basket. We left the remaining fruit for Meredith; we wouldn't be able to bring it into California, anyway.

We ate bananas and cinnamon toast for breakfast, then made our last-minute preparations to leave. Meredith and Steve stood in the driveway and waved goodbye as we left.

As planned, I rode with Kevin and Ammo in the CR-V. Once we were through Las Cruces and headed west on the 10, I said, "Kev?"

"Hm?"

"I killed someone."

He glanced sideways at me. "Who was trying to kill you."

"Yeah, but…"

"Who was a vicious child predator."

"Well, yeah…"

"Who was still alive when you were conked on the head. If you'd called 911 right then, he might have lived. You were prevented from saving him."

I sighed. "Okay, fine."

"I'm not trying to diminish your feelings. I'm just reminding you of the facts."

"That's the thing. My feelings."

"What are they?"

"Right now, I have this sort of free-floating anxiety."

"Perfectly natural."

"And… I don't feel as guilty as I think I should."

"Why do you think you should feel guilty?"

"I took a human life. I don't believe in the death penalty. It was wrong. Thou shalt not kill."

Another sideways look. "Since when does the Bible mean anything to you?"

"It doesn't. I just..." I punched him in the shoulder. "You're not helping."

He frowned at the road ahead of him, choosing his words. "When Jimmy was convicted of raping that kid, he was sentenced to life with a minimum of forty years before parole. He was supposed to still be in jail."

"Why wasn't he?"

"Gordon Wayne told us he'd escaped over two years ago. Walked away from a medium-security state prison in Las Cruces, straight into the desert. He'd never been found, and the consensus was that he was probably dead."

"Apparently not."

The corner of Kevin's mouth curled up. "Right. Look, I'm not a counselor. I know you'll work on this with Dr. Bibbins. But Jimmy was going to keep damaging people until someone killed him. I know it's controversial, but I don't believe for a second that child predators can be rehabilitated. He would never have stopped. If he hadn't come to your house, or if he'd killed you and gone back to the camp, he'd still be up there, raping kids. True?"

"True."

"Stop thinking about Jimmy. He doesn't deserve any more of your time. Think of all the kids you've saved. From being sent to that camp, from falling into Jimmy's clutches. Dozens of kids. Maybe hundreds. Who knows how long that camp would have continued to operate?"

I blew out a deep breath. "Jacob Baldwin helped. He tried to save himself and all the others."

"Yes. And if he'd died a half mile before your house, or a half mile after, he wouldn't have been found by you. Then Pastor Todd would have left you alone. Jimmy would never have heard of you. You were the perfect person to get justice for Jacob, and for all the other kids who'd suffered at that camp. You're the only person in Alamogordo who *could* have."

I thought of Travis Green, who'd be delighted to hear that Jacob's death served a higher purpose. "Maybe you're right."

He slugged me gently in the shoulder. "Haven't you heard? I'm always right."

We stopped at the rest area west of Deming to let Ammo out and drain the caffeine from our bladders. Liz walked Ammo while Kevin, Jon, Pete, and I visited the men's room, then Pete took the leash while Liz scurried to the ladies' room. He asked me, "How are you doing?"

"Okay. I wish my sunglasses were darker. Everything's too bright."

"I have an extra ball cap in the Jeep. That might help."

"Good idea."

We stopped and watched Ammo as he investigated a patch of ground. I said, "I talked to Kevin about killing Jimmy."

"Did it help?"

"I think so. I feel less anxious."

"Good." Pete squeezed my shoulder. "You shouldn't feel guilty about killing a child predator."

"I don't feel particularly guilty. I thought I should."

"*No*." His jaw was clenched. "They are the worst of the scum of the earth. They can't be rehabilitated. *Occasionally* they can be controlled."

"Like Terry Moynihan." The priest who'd abused Pete, who'd eventually married a guy who kept him on an extremely short leash.

"Yes. From what I heard about Jimmy, he would never have been controllable. He needed to be removed from society. Think of all the kids you saved."

"That's what Kevin said."

"Not to mention, you saved the state of New Mexico a *shitload* of money."

I snorted. "I hope they appreciate it."

"I'm sure they do. Should you call Dr. Bibbins now, while we have a signal?"

"Oh. Yeah."

I called and spoke to Dr. Bibbins' receptionist, who said she'd let the doctor know, and would get back to me with an appointment date and time. I thanked her, then remembered something else I needed to do, and typed out a text message.

Hi, Dr. Loomis, Pete and I are driving back to LA today. Thank you for the fruit basket and tell everyone else thanks too! See you soon.

I didn't get an immediate reply.

Once Ammo was fastened into the back seat of the CR-V, I climbed back into the passenger seat wearily and pulled the ball cap down over my eyes. "I'm sorry I can't drive."

"It's okay." Kevin smiled at me. "I like driving on open highway."

"I do too. Must be a remnant of our childhood travels across the country." Every summer until we were all in high school, we'd driven with Dad and Sarge from Oceanside to South Carolina, for our yearly family reunion.

"Probably. How do you feel?"

"Eh. My head hurts a little."

"Take some Tylenol."

"Yes, boss."

The closer we got to home, the better I felt. I didn't realize how much tension I was carrying in my shoulders until we crossed the Colorado River. When I saw the "Welcome to California" sign, I was flooded with relief.

I let out a deep breath and sagged in my seat. Kevin glanced over at me. "Finally feeling safe?"

"I guess. It's like a weight just lifted off my chest."

"This is a problem, huh?"

"Yeah."

"What are you gonna do?"

"No idea."

My relief doubled when we entered Los Angeles County, and quadrupled when we pulled into the driveway of Kristen's house. I felt like crying, and firmly instructed myself to hold it in. But when I walked into the house and saw my dad, Jeff, and Val, I couldn't stop the tears.

My dad wrapped me up in a hug. "It's okay, sport. You're safe now."

I nodded, sniffling. "That's why I'm crying. I think. Apparently, concussions make you emotional."

Jeff knelt and ruffled Ammo's ears. "He's okay?"

"He's been fine." I rested my head on Dad's shoulder and addressed Jeff... and Val, who was hugging Pete. "Why are you all here?"

Jeff straightened up. "I wanted to check on Ammo. And we wanted to check on you."

Val said, "You *scared* us."

"I scared *me*. Where are the boys?"

"In the pool with Samantha."

Dad squeezed my shoulders. "We thought we might have a family discussion."

"Oho." I looked around at them—Dad, Jeff and Val, Kevin and Kristen. "This is an ambush."

They all protested. Kristen said, "No, it's not. We just want to...clarify everyone's positions."

Pete sighed deeply. Exhaustion hit me like a hammer. Or maybe a lug wrench. I said, "Not tonight."

Kevin said, "No. Not tonight."

I said goodnight to the others. Pete carried the bags upstairs to our designated room and helped me get situated. He was fluffing pillows when my phone dinged with two text messages.

One was from Dr. Bibbins. ***Jamie, I'm so sorry to hear of your injury and troubles. You have an appointment with Dr. Nathaniel Sparks on Wednesday at 2:00 pm, and on Friday at 3:00 pm with me.*** She included Dr. Sparks' address, which was in the same UCLA medical office building where Dr. Bibbins herself was located.

The other text was from Dr. Loomis. ***Jamie, I'm glad you're home. I've only heard scraps about what happened, but I'm sure Liz will fill us in. I asked around, and no one here sent you a fruit basket, although we should have. Some mix-up, perhaps. Let me know if there's anything I can do for you.***

I said, "Huh."

Pete said, "What?"

"All those fruit baskets we got? One of them said it was from the library, right? But Dr. Loomis says she doesn't know anything about it."

"Maybe someone else from the library sent it?"

"She asked. No one did."

"That's odd."

"Yeah. Did we eat anything from that basket?"

He frowned. "I used apples from all of the baskets in the cobbler. And I know that we ate the bananas that were in it, and Liz and Meredith both ate oranges from it."

"Okay. No reason to be paranoid, right? Dr. Loomis said it was probably just a mix-up."

"She's right." Pete pulled the window shades down for me. "There you go. Ready for bed?"

"Yep." I hugged him tightly. "I love you."

"Love you too." He kissed me. "See you in the morning."

He turned out the light and closed the door behind him. I crawled into bed and stretched out but didn't drop off to sleep immediately.

If the library didn't send that fruit basket, who did?

Maybe the basket was meant for someone else and mis-delivered to us.

That was probably it.

I went to sleep.

Chapter 31

Tuesday, July 2

I didn't hear Pete come to bed, and I didn't hear him leave it in the morning. When I woke up alone the next morning, I found a text from Brian Cochrane.

Figured you'd be interested in this.

He'd included a link. When I clicked on it, I was routed to an article in the Alamogordo newspaper, dated this morning.

> **ALAMOGORDO - Two Alamogordo Police officers and an Otero County sheriff's deputy are on paid administrative leave after they were entangled in an officer-involved shooting yesterday that resulted in the death of two men.**
>
> **APD Officers Josh Smallwood and Benita Garza, and OCSD Deputy Randy Morales, were serving a search warrant at the home of Winston "Butch" Hicks, in the case of the attempted poisoning of a search and rescue dog earlier in the month. Smallwood, Garza, and Morales were invited into Hicks's home, where they were ambushed by Hicks and Cecil "Lumpy" Wells, who opened fire on the officers. Deputy Morales was struck in the hip; Officers Smallwood and Garza were unharmed and returned fire, killing both Hicks and Wells.**
>
> **The New Mexico State Police are investigating the incident. Deputy Morales's injuries are not considered to be life-threatening and he is expected to make a full recovery.**
>
> **Upon further investigation of Hicks's property, OCSD and the State Police found a large cache of weapons and ammunition, several tubs of rat poison, and approximately two dozen dogs being held in what animal control officials referred to as "deplorable"**

conditions. Hicks had been suspected of operating a dogfighting ring on his property, and evidence was found to support the allegation. Officials would not comment further.

I dropped my phone onto the bed and let out a deep breath. Ammo was safe. When we returned to Alamogordo—if we did—Ammo would be safe.

I hesitated for a moment, then texted Josh Smallwood. ***Hi, it's Jamie Brodie. Brian Cochrane sent me the article about your OIS yesterday. How are you?***

He answered immediately. ***Okay, thanks. On desk duty. You still in town?***

No, we're back in LA. How sure are you that you got the guy who poisoned Ammo?

Almost positive. Tobias Rice is comparing the capsules we found in that house to those in your yard. They look identical to the naked eye.

That doesn't mean someone else couldn't have the same batch.

True, but I think your dog is safe. You are too, most likely.

Wish I felt the same.

Don't give up on us yet. When are you moving here for good?

Unclear.

Tobias, Benita, and I are gonna do our best to ID and weed out anyone else that might have it in for you. Reckon it won't take us long.

Hope not. THANK YOU.

No problem. You take care.

Thx.

He returned a thumbs up.

I showered, carefully washing my hair while avoiding the shaved patch surrounding the stitches, then went downstairs, lured by the scent of bacon. At this rate, I was likely to turn into a side of bacon. I snagged a piece from the paper towel on which it was draining and went to the back patio, where I found my family gathered around the pool. Pete, Colin, Gabe, Samantha, Jeff, and Kevin were in the water with Ammo, playing volleyball.

Kristen and Val jumped to their feet. Kristen said, “Good, you found the bacon. What else do you want for breakfast?”

Val said, “I’ll make you cheese grits if you want.”

“Ooh. That sounds awesome.”

The two of them bustled into the house. Dad asked, “How are you feeling?”

“My head’s sore. But look at this.” I showed him the newspaper article.

He read it, nodding. “Do you suppose it’s your attempted poisoner?”

“Josh Smallwood thinks so.” I let him read our text conversation.

“Hm. Sounds like he thinks you’ll be safe, too.”

“We won’t be going back for a while. Maybe he and the others can uproot the bad actors before we do.”

“I’d prefer that.”

I huffed a laugh. “You and me both.”

I ate my fill of bacon, grits, and orange juice, while Kristen and Val fussed around me and pretended that wasn’t what they were doing. I appreciated their efforts. And I didn’t have the energy to mount a protest.

When I was done, Pete, Jeff and Kevin climbed out of the pool and dried off while Kristen and Val brought drinks to everyone. Pete sat beside me; the others ringed us in a semicircle.

I took a long drink of Coke then gingerly leaned my head back on the chaise. “Okay. Lay it on us.”

Dad said, “Obviously, we’re concerned about your eventual move to Alamogordo. We know that you love the house and have big plans for the garden. But it seems that you’re not safe there. And that’s not a condition that I can live with.”

I shot Kevin a glance. "We're not entirely safe here, either. Twenty percent of the hate crimes in LA are homophobic attacks." I paid attention to such statistics. Not to mention, the "boss" behind the conversion camp was in California somewhere. "And we have the Alamogordo cops and the state police looking out for us now."

Jeff said, "The house is a sunk cost. If you're thinking that you have to live in it because you spent all that money on it… that money is gone anyway."

"I don't think that. We want to live in the house because it's our dream house. We designed it exactly the way we wanted it. You've all been there. It's a fantastic house." Although I'd killed someone there. I wasn't ready to deal with that yet. "And Val, you of all people know how much work Pete has put into our plans for self-sufficient living. I'm not willing to toss that away. And I simply cannot deny Pete the chance to live in the same town as Steve does."

Kristen had a look on her face that I couldn't quite interpret. Skepticism? I said, "What?"

"Off topic. Tell you later."

I frowned at her but kept pressing my case. "The mayor came to see us. He was totally embarrassed by how we'd been treated. The police chief told the newspaper that we were the sort of residents that Alamogordo should welcome, not run off. We have the power on our side. I think…"

My phone rang. I glanced at the screen. "Oh, it's Meredith."

Dad said, "Better answer that."

I did. "Hey."

"Hey yourself. How are you?"

"Not bad. Val and Kristen have stuffed me full of eggs, bacon and grits. How are you?"

"I'm fine. I miss you guys, though."

"We miss you, too. What's up?"

"I just had a visit, here in the office, from Mayor Poole. He had news about the Holiness church."

"No kidding. Can I put you on speaker, so I don't have to repeat this?"

"Sure."

I lay the phone on the table. "Say hi, everyone."

Meredith laughed at the chorus of replies. "Hi, back. I was just saying to Jamie… the mayor came by the office just now. He says that the Holiness church is about to lose its lease. The property that it sits on is owned by a company called Cayaxa. I don't know who's behind that company, but whoever they are, they've suddenly decided that they want to build townhouses on that plot."

Everyone made "ooh" noises. Kevin said, "Suddenly, huh?"

"Yes. I suspect that Joey Norman might be involved in this somehow. Anyway, if the council votes to allow the proposed development, the church is going to be evicted."

Jeff asked, "Will they sue?"

"The mayor says that they only have about sixty members. They'll bankrupt themselves if they choose to sue."

Pete said, "That doesn't address Todd Jackson's church. It was those people who were harassing us."

Meredith said, "Actually, the guy who ran over Steve's mailbox is a member of the Holiness church. But as for Jackson's church… He's dead and literally half of the congregation is in jail. They don't own the land that their building sits on, either. The mayor said he's going to investigate the possibility of closing them down."

I asked, "Everything okay there?"

"Yes. Brian and Hannah are coming over this evening. We're gonna grill and *relax*."

"Sounds fun. Tell them hello for me."

"I will. I'll talk to you later."

I said goodbye and hung up, then turned to the others. "See? Our allies are dishing out consequences. We'll be okay."

Val said, "Just because their churches close, doesn't mean those people will leave town."

I said, "No, but these people aren't career criminals, and the cops are going to be watching them closely. And in the case of

Jackson's church, their leader is gone. Pete, feel free to jump in here at any point."

All eyes turned to Pete, who hadn't said a word yet. He was studying his fingernails. "Well. Val's right. You're all right. Maybe it's not the best place for us."

I turned to him in disbelief. "*What?*"

Dad raised an eyebrow. "Difference of opinion there?"

I stared at Pete, who was still looking down. "News to me."

My entire family exchanged "what the hell?" glances. Dad said, "Maybe you should clarify that."

I said, "Yeah. We should."

Jeff and the boys cleaned up from breakfast, then they, Val, and Dad headed home. Kevin went to work, dropping Sam off at UCLA on the way, which left Pete and me alone with Kristen. She jumped into the pool for a swim, providing the opportunity for me to probe Pete's thoughts.

We sat on the patio, watching Kristen glide back and forth through the water. I said, "Pete?"

"Hm?"

"Are you changing your mind about Alamogordo?"

He didn't look at me. "I don't know. Your family has a valid argument."

"Yes, but so do I."

"You do. I'm sorry. I'm just… I can't process all of this. The past few days… You could have *died*."

"But I didn't." I reached across the gap between our chairs and squeezed his arm. "Maybe you should see Dr. Bibbins, too."

He shook his head. "No. I just need a couple of nights of restful sleep. I'll be fine."

"Do you want to sell the house?"

He didn't respond for a moment. Then, "Not yet. Everything that happened is too fresh. I just… Right now, it's difficult to think about going back there."

"We'd planned to go back later in the summer."

He looked at me then. "Do you want to?"

"No. I want to stay here. I want to swim every day and go to the beach and hang out with Kristen and spend some time in Oceanside. I want to let this head injury heal and enjoy the rest of my furlough."

He smiled. "Sounds like a plan."

About a half hour later, Pete and Kristen exchanged places. He and Ammo jumped into the pool together and began playing a version of doggie water polo. Kristen rinsed the chlorine from her hair in the poolside shower then dropped into the chair beside me. "Did you and Pete talk?"

"Some. I think he's just as traumatized as I am, maybe more. And he hasn't been sleeping well. After a few more days, I think he'll come to his senses."

"Meaning that you still intend to live in Alamogordo eventually."

"Yes. You're the one who said that we needed to establish ourselves as Those Who Must Not Be Fucked With. If we don't go back, what message does that send?"

She huffed a laugh. "I must admit, Kevin and I don't feel as strongly that you shouldn't go back as your dad, Jeff and Val do. Kevin and Jon's encounters with the locals led them to believe that every official in that city is going to support you. And as Kevin said when we were there, he and I believe that the two of you can take care of yourselves. Mostly."

I showed her the news item that Brian had sent. "Josh Smallwood said he was going to take care of the poisoner, and he did. Now he says that he's going to take care of the rest of the homophobes. I believe him."

"How does he intend to do that?"

"Don't know. Don't want to know. Change of subject… What was that look about when I mentioned Steve earlier?"

She glanced at the pool, then gave me a look over her sunglasses and lowered her voice to a near-whisper. "Do not mention this to Pete."

"I won't."

"I'm not convinced that Steve is as excited about Pete moving to town as Pete is."

"Why?"

"I don't know him well, obviously, and I could be interpreting this entirely wrong. But my impression is that Steve is fine either way. If Pete lives there, great! If Pete doesn't live there, that's okay, too. Outside of his work, he has a 'whatever' attitude to the rest of his life that probably works well for him. But I doubt that's what Pete is expecting."

"No. He's not. Meredith herself described Steve as oblivious."

Kristen snorted softly. "Sounds about right."

"And he can be seriously insensitive." I described my conversation with Pete about Steve ignoring his history of abuse. "We both wondered how that worked for Meredith."

"Good question. Meredith seems to have her head screwed on right."

"I agree. She doesn't know about Pete's abuse, though, so she can't modify Steve's behavior in that area."

"Will Pete tell her at some point?"

I shrugged. "Up to him."

"Right." Kristen sighed. "Maybe Pete living there will change Steve for the better."

"Maybe." But knowing the Fergusons, I had my doubts.

Chapter 32

Wednesday, July 3

When I woke up the next morning, Pete was lying beside me, awake. He rolled up onto his side to face me and tapped me on the nose. "Hey."

"Hey, yourself. Happy birthday. And happy anniversary."

"Thanks. Happy anniversary to you."

"Thank you. What do you want to do this evening?"

"I hadn't thought about it. What do you want to do?"

If it was up to me to decide, then I'd decide. "How about this? We ask Sam to stay here at Kristen's one more night, but we go home. I don't really feel up to eating out. Let's get takeout, whatever you want to eat, and enjoy being alone in our own house."

He smiled. "Yeah. I'd like that."

"It's a plan, then. Think about what you want for dinner."

"I already know. Indian food. We haven't had any for a month."

"Perfect. Let's go home this morning."

"Sounds good. When is your appointment with the neuropsychologist?"

"Two o'clock."

"You think Kristen might make us a cake?"

"I bet she will, if we ask nicely."

Kristen readily agreed to bake a cake for us. She and Kevin would deliver it and our Jeep later this afternoon. We ate cereal for breakfast, showered, then loaded the dog and our luggage into the CR-V.

When we pulled into our spot under the deck at the townhouse, another wave of relief swept over me. Pete unfastened Ammo and allowed him to bound up the steps first. I followed more slowly, dragging my hand along the smooth wood of the rail.

I loved our house in New Mexico, but I loved this house, too.

Pete had just finished unloading the car when Meredith called. I answered, "Good morning!"

"Good morning to you! You sound happy."

"We just came home. To our house. I am happy. What happened at the city council meeting?"

"The variance passed unanimously, just like the mayor said it would. There were some people from the Holiness church there, protesting, but they don't own the land, so they're SOL."

"That's *awesome* news."

"It sure is. Oh, and I'm not sure what this means, but Brian said to tell you that Todd Jackson was named pastor at his church just under two years ago. He came from a church in Texas. Is that significant for some reason?"

I didn't want to think about Todd Jackson anymore. "Probably not. Thanks, Meredith."

"You're welcome. Tell Pete happy birthday!"

"I will. Talk to you soon."

I said goodbye and hung up. Pete said, "What did she say?"

I repeated her news. "Happy birthday to *you*, huh?"

"Why?"

"So long to those two churches. Which were probably the primary sources of our troubles." I hugged him, then tried to get him to dance a few steps. "Ammo's safe. *We're* safe."

"I guess."

I frowned at him. "You could have said that with more enthusiasm."

He dropped into one of the kitchen chairs. "I'm sorry. I just… It's been a long month."

"I know, hon." I kissed him on the head. "Let's unpack and forget about New Mexico for a while."

Our office, which was serving as Samantha's room, was a minor mess, but the rest of the house was clean. Pete helped me change the sheets on our bed, then he checked the fridge and cabinets and made a detailed grocery list while I called my dad with the update about the city council meeting. Pete would shop while I was at the doctor's office.

At 1:45, he dropped me at the UCLA medical office building then headed for Ralphs. I climbed the steps to the third floor and entered Dr. Nathaniel Sparks' waiting room, checked in with the receptionist, and sat.

Dr. Sparks himself appeared right at 2:00. "Dr. Brodie? I'm Nate Sparks. Come in."

"Call me Jamie. It's good to meet you." I followed him back to his office.

"You too, although I'm sorry it's under these circumstances." He gestured to an overstuffed wing chair in front of his desk, then sat behind his desk. "What happened?"

I explained the mechanism and aftermath of my head injury. "I'm mostly fine, I think, except that I have trouble concentrating. It's hard to read more than a few sentences, and I can't stand to drive. Everything is too bright. And I still have a dull headache, although that's a lot better since yesterday."

"Are you dizzy?"

"No, sir."

He nodded, taking notes. "What did they tell you about your MRI?"

"That it was normal."

"How long were you unconscious?"

"Um. Around an hour, I think? I'm not sure."

"Any loss of memory around the incident?"

"No, sir."

"From what you're telling me, I believe that you have a mild traumatic brain injury, which is the equivalent of a concussion. Have you had concussions in the past?"

"Two. One in middle school and one in college. I played rugby."

"Were you knocked unconscious?"

"No."

"Any residual from those?"

"No, sir."

"How long did it take you to fully recover from each of those concussions?"

"A week, maybe? Two at the most. I could ask my dad if he remembers."

"No, that's okay." He asked me a few more questions about my medical history, then set his notepad aside. "Let's do some testing and see where you are."

He led me to his lab, which was a cramped room holding a filing cabinet, desk, chair, and computer, with a second empty table and two chairs. He sat in one chair at the table and pointed me to the other. "I'm going to test you on several aspects of brain function." He opened a file drawer and extracted a packet of papers, then handed me a pencil. "Don't worry about speed on this first test."

I completed a series of varying tasks, involving sorting, colors, word recognition, memory, timed activity… all sorts of things. By the time we were done, I was tired.

"All right. As I suspected, your impairment is mild." He turned to a clean page on his pad and wrote something down. "Here are the URL, username and password for a website. You'll need to use a desktop or laptop, not your phone, and a mouse, not a touchpad. The site will provide a series of training exercises to complete. I want you to practice once a day, preferably mid-morning when you're most alert. I'll see you back in a week, and we'll repeat these tests. We'll keep it up until your tests show that you're back to normal function."

"How long do you think it will take?"

"Six to twelve weeks. I'm confident it won't be longer."

"Should I try to read? Will that help?"

"I'd recommend print rather than e-books. But yes, do try to read. Since reading is an important part of your life and work, it's just as vital to practice it as it is to complete the training on the website. Oh, and *absolutely* no contact sports for the next twelve weeks."

"Okay." I'd miss the first month of rugby practice. "What about running?"

He raised an eyebrow. “Do you feel like running?”

“Not really.”

“Then wait until you feel like it. Use some other method of exercise until you do.”

“What’s this therapy called?”

“Cognitive rehabilitation therapy. CRT. You can read about it, if you like. Come with me.”

He led me back to his office, where he handed me a booklet called *Mild Traumatic Brain Injury*.

“Thank you. I’ll make this my first reading assignment.”

“Excellent. I’ll see you next week.”

I had to wait outside the office building for nearly fifteen minutes before Pete pulled into the pickup circle. He said, “Sorry I’m so late. People kept calling and texting me.”

“Of course. It’s your birthday. Who called?”

“Steve, Meredith, Christine, and Stephanie texted. Your dad, Val, Lauren, Mel, Aaron, and Elliott called.” Lauren Fortner was our financial advisor; Melanie Hayes was our attorney; and Aaron Quinn and Elliott Conklin were Pete’s friends from his Santa Monica College days. “Mel asked how we were.”

“I suppose she’s been talking to Kevin.”

“Yeah. What did the doc say?”

I related the conversation and Dr. Sparks’ instructions. “Can we go to the Y to use the stair climber tomorrow? I think I could handle that okay.”

“Sure. When do you get your stitches out?”

“I have to get them checked this Friday at the urgent care center. I guess they’ll tell me then.”

“Then you can swim.”

“Feels like *months* since I’ve been in a pool, not just weeks.”

I really wasn’t making a statement on Alamogordo with that observation—there was a community center with a pool there that we could join if we wanted—but Pete gave me a sideways glance and didn’t respond.

At the house, Pete stowed groceries while I called in our order to the Indian restaurant around the corner. It would be an early dinner, but we hadn't had lunch and were both ravenous. When Pete came back from picking up our order, he said, "The Patels said they missed us."

The Patel family owned the restaurant. We'd come to know them well, since we ate there so often. "Aw. I missed them too."

"I told 'em. They gave us extra naan."

"Nice!" I pulled a corner from a piece of naan and popped it in my mouth.

He smiled at me as we sat down and divided the food between us. "You seem to be in a good frame of mind today."

"I am." I dug into my dal tadka. "Had a great doctor's visit, got a plan for cognitive rehab, it's our anniversary, it's your birthday, and the city of Alamogordo is dancing on the graves of our enemies. What more could I ask for?"

He spluttered. "That's one way to put it."

"You know what I mean."

"Yeah."

"I really am feeling better about New Mexico now. The cops and the city are gonna clean the place up before we get back. I could be wrong, but I think our troubles there are over. Of course, there's still no Indian food there."

"There is in Las Cruces."

"Yes. We can eat Indian food when we visit Target."

He sighed. "I hope you're right."

"About Target?"

"No, doofus. About our troubles being over."

"Josh Smallwood said that he and Tobias and Officer Garza were gonna make it safe for us. I believe him. He's already made it safe for Ammo."

At the sound of his name, Ammo scrambled to his feet and came to the table. Pete held up a finger. "No, Ammo. No people food."

Ammo looked sad and lay down at my feet. Pete said, "I doubt that anyone will mess with us again. As you said a few days ago, we are rich and powerful, and we've demonstrated that we are not to be fucked with. But what about those kids in Mandy's GSA? Will they get the same consideration?"

I tapped my fork on his plate. "Once we're there, maybe we can work with Mandy to make that happen."

His expression was pensive. "Maybe."

Kristen and Kevin arrived with a carrot cake about an hour later and stayed to have a piece with us, then left. Pete closed and locked the door behind them and turned to me. "It's too early for bed."

"Glass of wine on the upper deck?"

"Did you ask Dr. Sparks about drinking?"

"No. But what can one glass hurt?"

Once we were settled on the second-floor deck, I stretched out on the Adirondack chair with a satisfied sigh. "Aahhhh."

Pete chuckled and held his glass out. "Happy anniversary."

I clinked my glass against his. "Back atcha."

His phone rang, and he picked it up from the table. "It's my dad."

"Wishing his baby boy a happy birthday."

"Uh huh." Pete answered, "Hi, Dad."

While Pete chatted with his dad, I sipped wine and listened to the sounds of the city. Traffic, distant sirens, the occasional snatch of conversation. I heard our next-door neighbors, Drew Jemison and Holly Walton, come home and go into their house, commenting as they did that our cars were back. We'd check in with them tomorrow.

Pete's conversation didn't last long. When he said goodbye I asked, "How is he?"

"Says he feels great. Steph drove him out to the barn after dinner and he hung out while she fed horses." He gave me a sideways glance. "He didn't remember my birthday."

Whoa. "He admitted that?"

"Yeah. Chris reminded him." Pete sighed.

"Well, Chris told us that he'd been forgetting important things. It's a side effect of the new drug."

"I know."

I reached over and took his left hand in my right. "He loves you."

"I know. He said that."

"Good for him!" Jack didn't have a history of expressing affection to his kids. It was always a pleasant surprise when he did.

Pete squeezed my hand. "Maybe we shouldn't have gotten married on my birthday. Seems it's been all about my birthday and not about our anniversary."

I squeezed back. "As it should be. I told you, I've had a terrific day. And I'm expecting a terrific night ahead."

He grinned, the first real grin I'd seen from him in weeks. "One advantage to this house. We can shower together here."

I grinned back at him. "Yup."

And about a half hour later, that's exactly what we did.

I was running.

Running through the dunes of White Sands, the gypsum sliding beneath my feet. Someone was chasing me.

I stopped to catch my breath halfway up a dune and glanced back. A guy with a machete topped the dune behind me. He laughed at me as he slashed the machete through the air a couple of times. "You'd better run, cocksucker!"

I turned and scrambled up the dune I was on, then ran down the opposite side. I stopped again, halfway up the next dune, and waited.

Machete Man appeared at the top of the dune I'd just crossed.

I aimed the handgun I'd been carrying and shot him between the eyes.

I woke up in a sweat, heart pounding, gasping for breath. *Damn*. I'd have something to discuss with Dr. Bibbins tomorrow, for sure. I slowed my breathing and looked at the clock. It was 1:52 am.

Pete wasn't beside me. And Ammo wasn't in his bed.

There was light seeping in under the bedroom door. I climbed out of bed, opened the door, and tiptoed into the hallway. I didn't hear a sound. Samantha's bedroom was dark. I slipped down the stairs to the landing and peered down into the living room.

Pete was asleep on the sofa, a book open on his chest. The lamp on the end table behind him was shining on his hair. Ammo was curled on his auxiliary bed; he raised his head and thumped his tail as I crept down the second flight of stairs.

I padded to the sofa. Pete didn't really snore, but he was emitting the soft snuffling sounds that accompanied sleeping on his back. His Intro to Criminal Justice textbook was on his chest. I lifted it off gently, stuck a tissue in the page to mark it, and set it on the ottoman. There was a throw across the back of the sofa; I shook it open and spread it across Pete. He made an indistinct noise but didn't wake.

I stood there for a minute, watching him breathe, worrying about his irregular sleep patterns and his school plans, wondering if I'd ever be able to pry him from his laptop again. Wishing I knew how to help him.

I sighed and turned off the lamp.

Author's Note and Acknowledgements

Jamie's unpaid furlough is not based in reality. This year's budget for the state of California has increased the amount spent on the University of California system. UCLA has also raised tuition this year, for out-of-state students.

Thanks as always to my writing group: Bryan Seagrave, Chris Gebhardt, Dustin Weeks, Maggie Haridis, Michael Ivan Lowell, and Michelle Lee. Thanks to Stephanie Reppas and October Design Co. for another perfect cover. Thanks again to Megan O'Neill and Danny Haughn for taking me to Alamogordo, probably against their better judgment. □

Google Earth and Street View still don't show it, but there are now two houses on Pete and Jamie's street in Alamogordo. One is next door, to the north; the other is directly across the street. We are just going to pretend for now and the near future that those houses are not there.

My biggest thanks go to Chris Gebhardt, who has hashed out plots, corrected misconceptions, and edited every single one of the Jamie books for seven years now. Seems like forever ago that we started discussing plot points over lunch in a crappy break room, in a building that's now about to be torn down. How far we've both come…

And thanks to you, the readers, who have stuck with Pete and Jamie all this time.

Made in the USA
Middletown, DE
17 October 2020

22109232R00126